bât

bat

Sarah Withrow

BLOOMSBURY

First published in Canada by Groundwood Books Limited in 1998

First published in Great Britain in 2000 by Bloomsbury Publishing Plc
38 Soho Square, London, W1V 5DF

The moral right of the author and illustrator has been asserted
A CIP catalogue record of this book is available from the British
Library

ISBN 0 7475 4836 6

Printed in Great Britain by Clays Ltd, St Ives plc

1 2 3 4 5 6 7 8 9 10

*For all the young bats
and especially the original,
Kim Honey.*

1

"Come with me, Terence," Tom says.

He hardly ever calls me by my full name. It makes me feel even worse about him leaving. His German shepherd, Steel, is sniffing around Tom's duffle bag. He's getting his goober dog breath all over Tom's new T-shirts. Tom's mom has sewn little name tags into the backs of all his clothes — even his underwear. Like if his name wasn't on there some guy might steal his underwear.

Maybe I should steal it. Maybe he won't be able to go to stupid canoe camp if he can't find his underwear.

"Come on. Get inside." He smacks his duffle bag. It's half full.

Tom is always smacking things when he talks. He talks with his hands. Once he accidentally poked himself in the eye. That was good. For me, I mean. I'll miss him smacking stuff.

The duffle bag is filling up quickly. I can't believe he'll be gone for a month. He said come with me, but he won't stop packing the bag.

There's no room for me in there. I'd probably suffocate on his flathead geek sunhat.

"Take a chance for once, Terence. Just get in." He

puts his Walkman in the side pocket. The duffle bag is all bulging out. Steel is sniffing at it some more. Dogs are always happy — until you leave. They are happy until the second you close the door. If I were a dog, today would still be fun.

Steel turns and looks up at Tom like Tom is king of the universe. Tom reaches down to pat him and Steel lets a fart rip right into the duffle bag.

"No way am I getting in there now," I say. Tom grabs my head and tries to stuff it into the fart-filled bag. I get him by the back leg and bring him down hard on the floor. He jabs me in the stomach with his knobby elbow. I flip him against the door, and then his mom yells up, "Hey, hey, hey. You kids! I don't care what you're doing, just stop it."

We laugh until I feel like I have asthma because I can't breathe.

It starts to get quiet in Tom's room. I'm not going to be able to hang out here when he's gone. I can hear his parents talking downstairs. I can hear Steel's nails clicking down the hall. Tom is slouched up against the door. He's got his hands on his stomach from when he was laughing. His eyes are closed.

What am I going to do all summer?

2

It's kind of pathetic that I have to spend another summer hanging out in Wells Hill Park. My cousin, Elys, thinks I have so many friends. She says, "Go out and play," like there's some friend-filled magic playland just outside our front door. She believes my life is all wonderful just because I don't have to look for work.

I'm sitting on the hill with Rico chewing on the white ends of blades of grass. Rico's in the grade ahead of me. He hangs out with guys who spit on teachers' cars behind the school. Normally he wouldn't even give me the time of day. Summer changes all the rules. You never know who you'll end up chewing blades of grass with in the summer.

Anyway, that's what we're doing when Lucy comes over holding this big book.

"Want to hear about the Midget Employment Stabilization Board?" she growls. Tom says Lucy is an embarrassment to humanity. She draws these magic marker tattoos on her face. Like one day she has one that looks like a spider web, then the next day she's got one of a big flower, but you can still see the spider web underneath. And what's with that old blue sheet strung around her neck? It's like she thinks she's some kind of superhero. Plus she's got red hair, so she looks like a piece of red asparagus stuffed in a pillow case.

Still, you can't help listening to a story about something like the Midget Employment Stabilization Board, even if it is Lucy who's telling it.

We keep chewing grass and let Lucy go on.

"It says here this guy, Jim Moran, built these huge kites for midgets to fly in. But the whole thing was really a publicity stunt. Moran wanted the midgets to fly past windows in New York yelling at people through megaphones to buy these candy bars." In my mind I see Lucy hanging from a kite growling through a megaphone, with her stupid blue cape blowing in the breeze.

Lucy clears her throat and starts reading from the book. She tells about the cop that came along to stop Moran and the Midget Employment Stabilization Board.

"So the cop yells at them, 'You can't fly no midgets from no kites.'"

We crack up all over the hill when we hear that. At least, me and Rico crack up. Rico laughs so hard he starts coughing. I think something is going to come out of his nose, he's laughing so hard.

Except then Lucy starts yelling, "He shouldn't have made the midgets do all the flying for him. It isn't funny to be funny looking. And Moran shouldn't have called them midgets. He should have called them small people." That just makes us crack up harder.

"How would you like it if someone called you a midget?" she growls at Rico, like anyone would dare call Rico anything, he's so big. Rico looks like the world's biggest little kid. He's really tall and has biceps that look like someone sewed tennis balls into his arms. His face is kind of fat. Not like I'd say anything.

I don't get called names, either, but it's because my name is Terence and nothing rhymes with Terence. Also, I am completely ordinary. I have ordinary straight brown hair that's too long. And I've got an ordinary flat-as-a-pancake punched-in face, and a weenie chest that I hide pretty well under big T-shirts.

Maybe Lucy thinks it's better to be a weirdo than to be ugly. Being ordinary isn't exactly the same thing as being ugly, but it's close.

"I ain't a midget, Lucy Loser," Rico says. But he stops laughing after Lucy growls at him. He sticks a piece of grass in the corner of his mouth.

"No. You're Mr. Big Man," Lucy says. She has her hands on her hips.

"That's right, Loser. I'm Mr. Big Man. I like that," Rico says.

I'm still laughing about flying midgets, and the thought of Mr. Big Man sets me off again.

Then Lucy turns on me. "You are so insensitive." And the way she says it, and the way she looks at me in that get-up of hers, her eyes burning into me like tiny lasers…for a second I feel ashamed. For a second it's like I am a midget, or — what are you supposed to call them? I'm so out of it sometimes. I always do the wrong thing.

"I guess next to a small person, anyone could look like Mr. Big Man," she says to Rico. He pokes the air with his finger and opens his mouth, but nothing comes out.

Lucy rolls her eyes, slams the book shut and stomps off to hang out under the tree with the chess man. She takes the kite book with her, so I don't get to see the picture of that Moran guy.

"Who does she think she is — kite-queen or something?" Rico says. I pluck at the grass. He looks at me and snorts.

I've got to hand it to that Moran guy. Hardly anyone thinks up stuff like that anymore. Only weirdos think like that, and nobody *wants* to be a weirdo. Even loser weirdos like Lucy can come up with some good stuff sometimes.

I wish I could make my voice do that growl thing. It's kind of cool in a weirdo way.

3

When I get to the park after lunch the next day, I see Lucy in the middle of the field tying a couple of sticks together. I look around for Rico, but he must be up at the 7-11 getting a Slurpie.

"What are you doing?" I ask. She looks up at me.

"What does it look like?" She must still be burned about yesterday. I take a look at the junk she has in front of her: sticks, string, glue and this roll of Christmas wrapping paper with beady-eyed Santas on it.

"Are you making a present?" I ask.

She shakes her head. "Guess again." Then it comes to me.

I look around for Rico again and sit down.

"I've never seen a kite made with wrapping paper before," I say. She's got the cross bars made up already. She is so concentrated. Her tongue is sticking out of her mouth. Her hands seem to know exactly what to do. Why don't I think up things like making a kite?

"You just woke up this morning and decided to make a kite?"

"Yup," she says, but she doesn't stop working. I watch her put glue in the middle of the cross sticks. She hands it over to me, takes my fingers and works them around the middle of the cross where the glue is.

"Hold it like that until it dries." She rummages around in her dirty pink knapsack. She has to keep throwing her cape over her shoulder to keep it out of the way.

I do what I'm told. I hold still and look out at the park. Not a cloud in the sky.

Wells Hill Park has two hills in it altogether. We're talking foothills, as in they are about a foot deep. It has three sets of monkey bars — including one that looks like a big blue moon. It has swings, the baby kind, a tetherball stand and a small sandbox.

On the other side of the sandbox is a huge tree with a picnic table under it. Mostly it's used by the chess man. Every time you look over there he's play- ing chess. He has this white hair that's all greased back and these humongous horn-rimmed glasses. For a while I thought he was Lucy's father because I see her playing chess with him sometimes, but Rico says he's an old pervert.

The second hill goes down from behind this kid- die wading pool. Nothing goes on there. Even sun- bathers don't use it. It looks like a spot that's sup- posed to be for something only that something never happens. My whole summer's like that — one huge, long stretch of nothing.

"Boo!"

I almost drop the kite frame. I turn around and face

14

the monster shadow of Rico looming over me. "Got ya," he says and plunks himself next to me. "What are you fools up to?" Lucy won't even look at him.

"We're making a kite," I say.

"Out of that stupid wrapping paper?" He gets up, puts his foot on the wrapping paper and rolls it under his foot.

Lucy sighs.

"Why are you such a Moran, Rico?" she asks.

"What's that supposed to mean?" He takes his foot off the wrapping paper and Lucy grabs it away from him.

"It means go pick on somebody your own size. We're busy." Rico is quiet for a few seconds. Then he says, "Hey, Ter, you want to play some tetherball?"

The glue isn't dry on the kite frame yet. Lucy is busy with her other stuff.

"Maybe later," I say.

"What? You too busy helping Loser with her stupid kite?"

I look down at the kite, like it's the most fascinating thing I've ever seen, and pray for some cool thing to say to pop into my head.

"Can't you see we're busy here?" Lucy says. Rico looks at me, shrugs and goes to talk to the lifeguard at the wading pool. Rico calls her Boobacious, for two extremely obvious reasons. Only now I can't remember her real name, so I'm afraid to talk to

15

her in case Boobacious slips out.

"I bet he thinks she'll be his girlfriend or something," Lucy says. "She's way too old for him. He is so deluded. He couldn't see a fly if it were sitting on his eyeball."

I feel like I have to stick up for Rico.

"And you are all-seeing, right? You have x-ray vision or something?"

"No. Sonar," she says. She tucks her hair back behind her ear. She's drawn birds by her eyes today. Blue on the left and purple on the right.

"What are you supposed to be in that outfit, anyway?" I say.

"I'm not supposed to be anything. I *am* a bat," she says. "If you weren't so blind you'd see that right off. Or maybe you'd see it better if you were blind. Some things you see better with your eyes closed."

"Aren't you a little old to play pretend?" I say, but I'm already thinking about how she really could be a bat. It's like my cousin Elys says. If you believe it, it's not a lie.

"I'm old enough to do what I like." Lucy looks me straight in the eye. I'm not used to that. I don't know if I like it or not. When Tom talks, I look at his hands. His fingernails are always dirty, man.

"And you like being a bat," I say. She is way off. She's outside the universe, she's that far out.

"I am a bat. It's not really a thing you choose. It

chooses you." She's looking straight in my eyes. I look down at the kite again. She goes on in that growl of hers that you can't help listening to. "You know, in Finland, there are people who believe that their souls come out of their bodies when they are sleeping and fly around as bats." I imagine my soul flying out of my body and bashing into my bedroom window. Then I wonder if souls are naked and I guess I smirk because I hear Lucy growl, "You wouldn't understand, so just forget it. All right?" She looks pretty fierce. She can go on being a bat if she likes. It doesn't hurt me any.

"All right," I say. She makes me hold the frame as she loops string around the notched ends of the sticks. She ties the notches shut with smaller pieces of string.

"Okay. Now we have to put it on the paper," she says. She's barely looking at me the whole time. I hold the kite frame down and she cuts around it. We glue the flaps over the string and she pulls out the kite book to look at instructions. I still want to see that picture of Moran.

I look over her shoulder at the book. We just have to make the bridle and the tail now. We could be flying this thing in half an hour. I can't wait to see all those beady-eyed Santas staring down at me from the clouds.

"Oh, shoot," says Lucy.

"What?" Then I hear it. Daphne, Lucy's big sister, is hollering for Lucy.

"Just ignore it," she says. It's hard to ignore some-one hollering "Lucy Goosey." Lucy bites her lip and starts putting her stuff back in her knapsack. "She's never around except when I don't want her to be."

I look over at Daphne. It's like she's allergic to coming right into the park to get her sister. It's like those five extra steps are too much work for her.

"Okay, I gotta go. We'll fly it tomorrow in the ravine." Lucy isn't asking me. She's telling me. I nod and watch her carry the kite out of the park. As soon as she sees Lucy is coming, Daphne turns and starts walking. Lucy turns to wave at me and then runs after her.

I guess we're friends now.

I wonder why Daphne doesn't actually come into the park when she comes to get Lucy. She must like hollering.

I've seen Daphne flipping burgers behind the counter at Fatso's. She looks kind of like what Lucy should have looked like if God had gotten her face right. Lucy's nose is all long and sharp and her fore-head goes up too high. Daphne's face looks like it's had those pointy bits sanded down. Her hair is dark-er, more brown than red. It hangs straight and moves in one long shining piece when she walks. Lucy looks like she's got a red porcupine sitting on her head. Daphne's almost perfect. She's got that big birthmark by her eye, but it looks like it belongs there. Her voice is round and smooth.

I like to hear her hollering for Lucy. Sometimes I wish I had a dog, just so I could lose it and holler for it. I'm completely serious about that.

On my way home I think about what Lucy said about bats and seeing with your eyes closed. I think I know what she means. I see all sorts of things. I see gaps in the way things happen, the huge stretches in time with nothing and no one to carry you to the next real moment. Like this big long one now between making kites and dinner time. Nothing to do again. If Tom were here we could play some cards. If Rico wasn't talking at Boobacious, I'd let him beat me at tetherball.

I guess I'll go home and watch TV.

I wonder what a bat does at home?

I get home and my cousin Elys is there staring at an open fridge.

"Spying on Mr. Mustard?" I say. I swear, she spends more time looking in our fridge than I spend watching television. She hangs around our place a lot. Elys's mom took off to France when Elys was seven, so she sort of adopted my mom and now she practically lives here half the time. I guess she's supposed to be keeping an eye on me. Mom's always working late or doing dinner with this guy Farley.

"You got any cheese?" Elys asks. She leans into the fridge and pokes a couple of jars like they might be full of pickled spiders or something. The labels are all worn off and Elys has to squint to read them.

She has had the same pair of pink-rimmed glasses since forever. The problem is her head has grown a lot in the past few years and now her glasses make her eyes look like pinholes. The arms of the glasses cut into the side of her head. She spends a lot of time rubbing the side of her head and getting her fingers caught in that mess of curly mophead she has.

Elys graduated from the University of Toronto last year and hasn't been able to get a single job. She even applied to be a house painter. She almost applied to McDonald's, but my mom said Elys's job search attitude was pathetic and she ripped up the application.

I grab a banana and head for the TV. Mom never gets home before 8:30. The cable channel says it's only 4:48. See what I mean by gaps?

I can guess the ending to every single show on the tube. I can't remember the last time I made a bad prediction.

You would think it was satisfying to be right about the endings of things all the time. It's not. Knowing how everything is going to turn out — it's the worst thing I can think of.

4

Lucy has new kites flying out the sides of her eyes today. One is orange and the other is green. You'd think she'd make them match, at least.

We're going to fly the kite in the ravine behind St. Clair West subway station. It's pretty close to the park, but it feels like it's far away because I never walk that way.

"You ready?" Lucy says when I get there. Rico is standing beside her holding the kite. It's got a tail on it with pieces of black garbage bag tied to it.

"Yeah, you ready to see if this loser kite flies?" says Rico.

"He brought a spool of kite line with him, so I said I'd let him watch. He's not allowed to fly it, though." Lucy does not look happy.

"Fly? There's no way this loser kite is going any-where but down," Rico grins. "And I plan to be right there when it crashes and burns."

"Where'd you get the kite line?" I ask.

"What's the difference? I got it, didn't I? Loser thought she could fly a kite with wool. Ha!"

As we climb down the hill beside the subway station, Lucy points out the bridge that spans the ravine.

"Bats live under bridges," she says. "They like it where it's dark and they won't be disturbed by human beings. It's not hard to disturb a bat. Bats can hear bugs walk. Humans can wreck a bat's hibernation by just walking in a cave. How would you like it if someone came into your house and scared you out of a deep sleep? Never mind that it takes you forever to get back to sleep again and you might not have enough body mass to make it through the whole winter anymore because some stupid human made you waste it all on being freaked out. Humans don't care about bats. They don't even know when they're killing them."

She's on about the bat junk again. Still, I wonder if there are any bats living under the bridge.

Where does Lucy get all this information anyway? I want to ask her about it but not with Rico around. He has a way of making every conversation be about him. Even the kite is about him now.

*

The ravine is all overgrown and wild. The grass comes up to my knees in some places and there's all these little purple flowers around. There's never anybody down here. It has this feeling about it, like it's been forgotten by the rest of the city.

When we get to the middle of a clearing in the ravine, Lucy licks her finger and holds it up to see which way the wind is blowing. Pretty soon we're all holding spitty fingers up in the air. Then Rico licks his whole forearm to get a more accurate reading.

"I can't feel nothing," he says and waves his arms around. "Wait! I feel the wind beneath my wings. Arrrooooo!" He circles us, flapping his arms like a madman. What a goof. Why couldn't it have been Daphne who found the kite line?

"Where's your sister?" I ask Lucy.

"Why?"

"Isn't she supposed to take care of you?"

"Yeah. Right. Where's *your* sister then?"

"I don't have one."

"Lucky you. I'm gonna choke if I have to eat one more Fatso burger for dinner. I must be a vegetarian bat."

I'm about to ask her more about the bat thing, but Rico is in our face flapping his arms.

"Do you want to fly this kite or not?" Lucy asks, and Rico quits his bird impersonation.

It's Lucy's bat cape that proves conclusively which way the wind is coming. The stupid costume turns out to be useful.

Rico takes the kite and runs around, pumps his arms for speed, but mostly looks like a scared chicken.

"Stand still a sec," Lucy yells at him.

The kite keeps slamming Rico in the back of the

head. He won't stop running even though he's getting slammed in the back of the head and is sweating down the back of his shirt.

"Rico," Lucy hollers. Rico isn't listening. You can tell from the way he isn't looking at us that he is determined to get that kite in the air before Lucy has a better idea of how to do it. If Tom were here he would holler at him to quit being such a running-around-like-a-scared-chicken dork.

"Hey, Rico," I holler. But I don't holler loud enough and Rico's still running. I open my mouth to holler again, but this time Lucy takes the cue and we yell out together, "Hey, Ricoooooo."

Finally he stops. Lucy grins at me.

"I can't get any wind under it," he says between breaths. "I knew that thing wouldn't fly, man." He bends over to catch his breath, and I take the kite from him. I look at Lucy's cape to see which way the wind is blowing. I lift the kite above my head and angle it into the wind. I can feel the wind pulling it out of my hands. I stand on my toes and let the kite slip out of my grip and into the sky. Lucy gets busy trying to control the spool.

"Get out of town," Rico says. "I don't believe it. No way." He falls over onto his back and sticks a piece of grass in his mouth.

"No problemo," I say and go to help Lucy with the line.

We all take turns holding the line. The kite looks cool when it's in the air. There's something about flying things and the way they seem to find invisible paths in the sky. Flying a kite, even a dorky Christmas wrapping-paper kite, is as close to flying as you can get. You can feel the sky pulling you up. You can feel yourself nearly get swallowed by the sky.

Rico is lying on the ground eating grass and watching the kite. He looks a little disappointed. The thing goes higher and higher. For sure it's going to reach a cloud. I want it to poke the edge of a cloud and make it start raining. I want it to rain on Rico's head. It could happen. You never know.

The kite line strains through my hands.

"The line cuts into your hands," I say to Lucy. She wraps her bat cape around her hands and takes the line from me. "Thanks," I say. Now that we've got the thing up, it's never coming down. It's like it's a bird and we're holding its tail and it's trying to get away from us by flying to the stratosphere. No way are we letting go. No way is Lucy letting go. No escape for that bird, man.

We can't get the thing to reel in, it wants to get away so bad. You can feel the line stretching, and, since it's our only line, we don't want it to break by forcing it too much. I'm secretly rooting for the kite. I want it to get away, to take off forever into the world of wind.

Lucy figures out a way to get it to do tricks by tugging on the line. When it swoops, Lucy swoops with it. The kite zigs and she zags. It's like Lucy and the kite are dancing. She teases it so it looks like it's about to nose-dive straight onto the bridge over the ravine and die under the wheels of some car.

Rico jumps to his feet and yells, "Timber! She's coming down."

"Don't say that!" screams Lucy. She seems really angry all of a sudden. I swear I see tears in her eyes. She tugs at the line furiously with this scrunched, mad look on her face.

At the last possible second, the kite sweeps up into the air and makes me gasp with how much it wants to go up and away. Lucy looks relieved. I watch a smile crawl back to her face. She looks so different when she smiles. Most of the time she looks kind of cross.

I wonder if Lucy's bat nature means she knows about flying. I wonder if her soul leaves her body at night and flies around as a bat like she said. Could be true. You never know.

"What's it like to be a bat?" I ask her.

I can feel my heart knocking against the back of my throat. I didn't mean to ask her straight out like that. I've been thinking more about what it would be like to be something else instead of me. Like Lucy is a bat. She said it was something that chose her. I want to know if it was in a dream or what. I have twice flown in dreams, but I have never been anyone else but me in one.

Just once, I'd like to be someone or something else. Just for a day, or an hour, or a minute.

I used to think I wanted to be Tom, but now I think — and I know it's crazy — I'd rather be a bat. Something that escapes into the night sky like a kite that snaps off its line as the sun's going down. Something that flies, almost invisibly, through dark and quiet air.

She looks at me and then up at the kite. Maybe she didn't hear me. It's a private thing, wanting to be something else. I don't have any business asking about Lucy's batdom. I'm almost relieved she didn't hear me.

"I see things upside-down," she says. I barely hear her say it. It's like she's telling it to the kite spool. She's usually loud, louder than Tom even. Not now.

I take a step closer. She's still got her bat cape around the kite line.

"Upside-down? How do you mean?" I want to know now.

"It's like I know things are supposed to look one way, but I keep seeing them the exact opposite. Bats sleep upside-down all day long. Me, too. And when I close my eyes at night and just listen…that's when

I'm most awake. That's when I know exactly what's what."

"When you're dreaming?"

"No. Before sleep. Like when my mom gets home and before my dad goes to work — he works the night shift at the bakery. They don't talk, but you can tell what's going on. You can listen to the spaces."

"I don't get it." That's what I say, but the second after I say it I *do* get it. It's like those gaps I keep noticing.

"Never mind," she says. "Forget it." She shoots a look at Rico to make sure he's not listening. The guy's busy rolling up the sleeves of his T-shirt.

"I think I know what you mean," I say. I want to get it in before Rico gets tired of checking out his tan. "It's like when people say they're fine, but you can tell they aren't. It's like the way people smile at you when they want you to get out of their way. Right? Like when you feel like something is supposed to be happening, but something else happens instead."

Like when your mom says she'll take you to a movie on Tuesday night but your cousin comes to pick you up instead, and you aren't supposed to say anything about it because you're getting to see the movie, aren't you? Like when you make a point of asking about summer camp and then school's out and you find yourself not at camp but flying handmade Santa Claus kites with Rico the spit-boy and a bat in a ravine.

"Yeah. Almost," she says. "You know anything about bats?"

"A little."

"I have a book. I'll bring it tomorrow." She hands me the spool. "Here. My hands hurt. Bats use their wings to hold things and scoop things. But we have to be careful not to get holes in our wings."

We work it so that her bat cape is tied to the line to protect my hands. I am very careful with the cape. I don't know what Lucy would do if it got a hole in it.

She has to have her back to the kite to make it work. The cape pulls straight up the line as the kite flies even higher.

"Wheeeee," Lucy sings. "I'm flying now. I knew this cape was good for something." Which is funny, because I was just thinking that.

"That is the dorkiest thing I've ever seen. You are one twisted loser," Rico says. He stares at us, shakes his head and throws up his arms, but I can tell he wishes he were on the end of the line watching Lucy's cape bubble in the breeze.

Like I said, these weirdos sure come up with some good stuff sometimes.

No way would Tom get this in a million years.

5

I'm late going to the park the next day because of Elys. Turns out my mom was having a sleepover date with Farley, so Elys stayed to take care of me, only she didn't do so good a job because she slept in.

She should get up on time at least.

"It's not like you have anything better to do," I tell her.

"Thanks for reminding me, kid."

"You have one thing to do all day and you can't even do that."

"Yeah, yeah, yeah. Who cares? I don't remember signing on as your alarm clock, Terence. I'm doing your mom a favor, okay? Don't give me any grief."

"You're not even dressed yet."

"That's *my* business." She takes a sip of coffee and looks at me. Her eyes look like little black marbles when she doesn't have her glasses on. "Didn't you say you had somewhere to be?"

"If I miss kite-flying today, I'm sticking cheese slices in your slippers tomorrow," I yell and slam the door behind me.

*

When I finally get to Wells Hill Park, Lucy is swinging on one of the baby swings, sitting on top of the cross bar. She's way up there where the chains start to go slack. Her bat cape billows out behind her. You can't go much higher than Lucy is right now.

Now that I'm here, I feel strange about yesterday. I don't see the kite anywhere and, for some reason, I can't quite look at Lucy straight. It makes my heart go all funny.

I see Rico hanging out with Boobacious by the wading pool. I think I'll go join them.

I'm careful not to look at Lucy. It's like, if I don't see her, she won't see me. I map out a route through the playground that takes me past the swings, but not right toward them.

I can't really be friends with a weirdo like Lucy anyway. Yesterday was just a freak thing. If Tom ever found out, man, I'd never hear the end of it. Tom's my real friend. If he were here, we'd be playing frisbee with Steel. Tom always knows what to do, and I just do what he does. Tom says that's because I'm easy-going. I think it's because I'm clueless.

I'm halfway across the playground when I see Lucy heave herself off the moving swing. She lands right smack beside me.

"Holy," I say. I still can't look at her.

"Bats are the only mammals that fly," she says. She looks me straight in the eye and I want to look away but I can't. I remember seeing in this vampire movie how the vampire mesmerized his victims with his eyes before sucking their blood.

"Are you a vampire?" I ask.

"Are you whacked in the head?" she says. "There's no such thing as vampires. Don't talk crazy talk."

What do you do when a human girl bat tells you not to talk crazy talk?

"I guess that means the chess guy isn't a vampire pervert then." She hauls back and socks me in the arm. It hurts something fierce, and I feel my eyes tearing up. I have to tilt my head back a little to keep them from falling out.

"Ow." I say it sarcastically, though I'm blinking back tears. I rub my arm. She left a mark.

"You can't talk that way about my friend. You don't even know him. Friends stick up for friends, but I guess you don't care about loyalty. You walked right past me like I wasn't even here. You should treat your friends with respect, Terence. You're supposed to be smart."

How would she know that? She was in a class way at the other end of the school last year. She was in the cootie class with the dumbheads and the problem kids.

"I don't respect violence," I tell Lucy. I wonder why she was in the cootie class, because she isn't a dumbhead. Must be the outfit.

"No? What do you respect?" She's turning on me again. "Huh? Lifeguards with big boobs?"

I can feel my face flush. I'm dying. I don't even know what to say, I'm so dead. I decide to keep to the original plan of heading for the wading pool. There's a water fountain there. I am suddenly so thirsty.

I get to the water fountain and gulp down a river. The water is so cold I can feel it going all the way down into my stomach and freezing up my insides.

Lucy's eyes slowly come into view on the other side of the drinking fountain. She has multi-colored magic marker squiggles fanning out from the corners of her eyes, like a cat.

"Sorry," she says. She looks over at Rico and Boobacious. Rico's resting back on his hands, trying to look casual. "I know what you guys call her. But it's really none of my business if you want to act like jerks." She stands up to full red-asparagus height and sticks out her hand. She wants me to shake it.

"I shouldn't have hit you," Lucy says. "Bats don't hit." Her hand is still out there waiting for me to do something with it.

"Or draw blood?" I say.

"Or draw blood…at least the kind of bat I am doesn't. I'm a brown bat. A microbat. We echolate. We eat mosquitos. I guess some mosquitos have blood in them, but it's not the blood we're after."

I wonder if Lucy has ever really eaten a mosquito.

I take Lucy's hand and shake it. She's got a hand-shake that means business. I can't help noticing she bites her nails. Me, too. It's hard to explain the satis-faction of nail-biting to anyone who doesn't indulge. It's like a secret club that lots of people belong to, adults included, but nobody ever says anything about it. Nail-biters notice other nail-biters. We know about each other's secret life of click-click chew. It's not a proud thing, but it is a bonding thing.

Tom doesn't bite his nails. I don't hold it against him. In fact, Lucy is the only friend I have who bites his nails. I mean, her nails.

"I brought that book," she says and starts walk-ing toward the picnic table under the big tree by the sandbox where the chess-playing pervert sits. He's in the middle of a game with a black man who is wearing a blue suit blazer even though his shirt is undone underneath. I'm afraid to follow Lucy because it means hanging with these guys.

"Wait," I say. Lucy doesn't hear me. She turns around and waves for me to come. I look over at Rico, but he's busy telling some story to Boobacious, who looks totally bored. I have no choice but to fol-low Lucy.

As we get close to the table, the black guy holds one hand up and another to his lips. The guy with the white hair nods at Lucy but doesn't smile. I hear something ticking. They're playing with a clock.

Lucy squats down and puts her elbows on the table. I can see her eyes bobbing over the chess pieces.

All I know about chess is that the bigger the piece is, the more powerful it seems to be.

The black guy shifts a pointy-headed piece diagonally across the board, picks off a pawn (I know a pawn when I see one), and slams his hand down on the clock.

"Exposed horse," Lucy says. The white-haired guy nods.

"I didn't see that," the black man says. "I should have seen that. Luscious, you have got to stay here and help me out."

"Can't stay, gotta go," says Lucy.

"People to see, things to do?" the white-haired man says. He doesn't even look up from the board.

"Aren't you going to introduce us to your friend, Luscious?" the black guy says. The white-haired man looks at me for the first time. He does something to the clock so that it doesn't tick anymore.

"This is Terence." Lucy flicks her thumb at me. I don't know if I should try to shake their hands, or what. I half lift my hand to see if that's what is supposed to happen. When they don't do anything, I just sort of wave it across my chest.

"Hi," I say. Lucy is digging for something in her knapsack under the picnic table. The men are checking me out.

"Is he a bat, too?" the white-haired man asks. He's looking out over these huge glasses of his. If it weren't daytime, I would think he was a vampire for sure.

"Yeah, you check him out? What does his father do?" says the black guy.

"Does he have a cool car?" says the white-haired man.

"Does he treat you good?" says the black guy.

"Is he worthy?" says the white-haired chess-man.

"I don't know. Yes. I don't know. No. Yes. I don't know." Lucy counts off her answers on her fingers. I lose track. "Terence, this is Russell," she says, pointing to the white-haired man. "And this is Martin. Martin plays chess at lunch on Fridays because no one buys insurance on Fridays because Fridays make people feel invincible. And Russell has nothing better to do." Just like Elys, I think.

"I resent that," says Russell. "There is nothing better to do than play chess. Martin, can you think of anything better than playing chess?"

"Only one thing I can think of," says Martin. He winks at Russell, then turns to Lucy "And that's being a bat." He starts making this beeping sound

36

and waving his arms around. Lucy pushes on his arm, but ends up going up and down with it as Martin keeps waving. We all start laughing. Then Lucy leans over the table and bangs the clock. It starts ticking again.

"Keep your eye on the horse," Lucy tells Martin.

"Knight, Lucy. It's a knight," Russell says.

"I just call 'em like I see 'em," says Lucy.

"And she does see 'em," Martin says, shaking his head. "See you later, Luscious. Nice to meet you, Terence." I give another little wave as we leave the table. Russell doesn't even look up. It's like when that clock is on, there's no world beyond that chess board.

Lucy sits down on one of the benches on the other side of the tree and pats the spot beside her. Guys don't do stuff like pat the seat beside them. It's an unwritten rule. I keep forgetting Lucy's not a guy. Not that she looks like a guy. I just don't feel like I'm hanging around with a girl when I'm with her. I know I felt strange about her this morning, but that had more to do with her being a weirdo than with her being a girl.

"You play chess?" I say. "It looks pretty compli-cated."

"No big deal," she says. "I'll show you sometime. You only have to know two things to play chess: one, you have to know how all the pieces move, and, two, you have to kill the king to win."

"What's the horse?"

"I told you, I'll show you another time. You can't explain it without the board. Now, did I lug this thing all the way over here for nothing?"

I'm not really all that interested in the bat book. I wonder what Lucy did with the kite. I want to go kite-flying again so we can talk some more while we fly the kite. I want to know what Lucy hears at night, and if it's anything like what I hear. The sound of my mom's key in the lock when she comes home after midnight, the quiet of everything else in the house against the chug of traffic out on Bathurst Street.

Lucy flips the book open. There is a picture of a bat with its wings spread out. Its ears are gigantic and its nose looks like someone hit it in the face with a shovel.

"Our fingers make up the bones in the wing," says Lucy. "The wing is actually a membrane that covers all the fingers except the thumb. We use the thumb for climbing. The membrane is so thin, it's almost translucent. Like when you hold a sheet up to the light and you can see through it. You can see our bones right through the wings."

We? I know Lucy thinks she's a bat. But does she really think she's got a bat body? I look her straight in the eye to see if she's on the level. She looks at me, but then turns back to the book.

"Bats have difficulty walking because our legs are

too weak to support the weight of our bodies."

"What do you mean?" I say.

"You heard me, Terence. We can hardly walk from being too heavy for our little feet."

"You mean *real* bats can hardly walk," I say. She slams the book shut.

"I told you. I *am* a bat." She closes her eyes. "You still don't get it, do you? I thought you got it." I want to talk about gaps, so I give.

"I get it. I get it. You see the world upside-down. You have trouble walking because you're too heavy for your feet." And then this flash goes off in my head. I know about being too heavy, the same way I know about hearing gaps.

I start talking quickly. "It's like that for me some mornings. On the weekend, when there's absolutely nothing to do, and I can't sleep in no matter how hard I try. I feel like I'm a million pounds getting out of bed. I can hardly make it to the couch before I have to keel over again. I can hardly carry myself to the fridge." I can't believe I'm telling her this. The thing is, I know she understands. Tom might understand if you explained it to him for an hour. Rico would never get it.

I look up at Lucy. She's boring a hole right through me with her laser eyes.

"You might be a bat," she says. "I'm not sure. We'll have to do some more checking." She looks at me with those piercing eyes and it's like she's trying to see my bones.

"What kind of checking?" I know it's crazy, but as soon as she says it, I want more than anything to be a bat. I want to belong to batdom. I want my wings, man. I want to fly.

"I don't know," says Lucy. "I *know* I'm a bat. It's like knowing how to chew. You don't think about it, you just do it. I just am a bat."

"But you weren't always one, were you? You said it was something that chose you. How did you know?"

I want to be chosen by bats. I want to be a bat like Lucy.

"You know, we didn't always live in an apartment," she says. "I used to live in a house. I miss it. But anyway…in our old house on the Escarpment we had bats in our attic. My parents didn't know about them for a long time. Not until…" She stops for a moment. "I could hear them through my closet. I could hear them come home in the early morning. I woke up just to hear them come in. The trap door to the attic was in my closet, but the door to it was missing, and I could see straight up through to the rafters. One day, I piled a bunch of old telephone books in my closet and got up there. The bats were roosting in the corner, all huddled up together to keep warm, all hanging upside-down. They were no bigger than my hand. I went up to visit them every day. I had to be very quiet so that I wouldn't disturb the other bats. For a long time, my parents and Daphne never knew. For a long time they thought I was normal."

She looks at me to see if I'm paying attention. She picks at a piece of paint on the bench, which is a challenge when you don't have any fingernails. I start picking at the bench, too.

"I liked it up there. It was dark, and nobody knew where I was. I found some old rope and I used it to make a slip knot. You know, like a noose. I tied it to one of the rafters near the corner where the bats slept. I got a stool from the kitchen and slipped my feet through the knot, then I let myself go. I hung upside-down like that a few times. The rope burned my ankles, and Mom asked about the stains on my socks."

I get a really good chip of paint off the bench and hold it up for Lucy's approval. She nods. "Anyway, the point is I didn't do it because I enjoyed it. I did it because I had to do it. It felt like I was falling, swinging upside-down like that. I had to know what it was like to feel like I was falling. Like Timber."

She stops again suddenly. I remember how she got upset when Rico yelled "Timber" the other day.

I don't know what to say. I keep picking at the paint on the bench. I wonder what it would feel like

41

to hang loose from the ceiling. I never even thought of doing anything like that. All this time I've been watching trashy television shows I could have been hanging upside-down instead.

I want to say how cool it is to think of doing something like that, but the words don't come out of my mouth. I wonder if Tom would think it's cool to hang upside-down.

"What did you do with your hands when you were hanging upside-down?" I ask.

"I tied the cape around my waist and sort of let them hang folded up. Here, I'll show you." Lucy walks over to the set of monkey bars that looks like a big blue planet. She climbs almost to the top and lets herself hang upside-down. Her spiky hair fans out around her head. She takes the ends of her cape and ties them tightly around her waist. She folds her arms up into the sheet and sort of shimmies the corners of the opening over her elbows, so that she's all tucked in. She closes her eyes and lets herself go limp.

"Cool," I say. I expect Lucy to jump down, but she doesn't. "All right, I see how it works." I say. She doesn't respond. It's like she plans to hang there all day. "Lucy?" I begin to walk backwards. Maybe she'll think I've left and give it up.

No such luck. Rico comes blazing into the playground on his bike. He slams his brakes and skids right up beside me. I try to make like I'm just being casual, but it's too late. He's already seen Lucy.

"Hey, what's with Loser?" Rico asks. I shrug. "Is she doing some escape-artist routine or something?" He yells this right at the monkey bars.

Rico ditches his bike and climbs up the outside of the planet. He perches at the top. He looks at me and waggles his eyebrows.

Oh, no.

He grabs Lucy's ankles and unhooks them so it's only him holding her up. I see her eyelids flutter but she doesn't open them.

"Got you now, Loser," he calls down to her. "Wakey, wakey. It's time to die." He doesn't seem to have a really good hold of her legs. Her head is coming close to banging against the bars. Her face is perfectly calm.

I'm mentally begging Lucy to smarten up and quick. But her face is empty. She looks more peaceful than before Rico showed up.

"You're getting heavy, Loser. I can't hold on much longer." Rico has his teasing voice on but I can tell he really is having trouble holding on to Lucy's feet. Plus, he's grunting. He's not balanced properly on top there.

I feel my heart pounding. I remember what Lucy said about loyalty. Does that mean trusting a friend not to let some goof drop her on her head?

"Come on, Lucy," I say. "He really is losing it." Rico loses his grip on her legs for a second and Lucy falls an inch. Her face shows no fear. It is like she is in some kind of trance.

"It's wake-up time, Loser," Rico grunts again. You can hear the effort in his voice. "Better grab onto something or you're going to smash down on your head."

I run over and start climbing through the bars. Rico loses it before I can get to Lucy, and the best I can do is stick my feet out under her head before she falls straight down on it. Only she doesn't. She has somehow managed to hook one of her feet around the pole so that her head hangs about four inches off the ground. She opens one eye, grins at me and closes it again.

"The hind feet of a bat are incredibly strong. They've even found dead bats in caves, still hanging upside-down," she says.

"I thought you were a dead bat," I say. I look up through the bars at Rico. He's trying to figure out what happened to save him from being a murderer.

"Some Losers just won't die," he says and jumps off the top of the monkey bars and lands rolling in the dust. "Come on, Terence."

"Come on where?" I say. Lucy is still hanging from the bars. She's got her eyes shut again. How long will she keep this up?

"Come on, already," Rico says. "I've got something to show you." I look at Lucy for some sign of life. "You don't want to hang with that Loser, do you?" Still, Lucy does nothing. "She's not your girlfriend, is she?"

No, no. I guess she's not. And I guess we aren't flying the kite today, either.

6

Rico takes me out of the park. I feel nervous about leaving Lucy. We wander up to St. Clair. We can't move too fast because Rico is walking his bike. The farther away we get, the less it seems to matter that some kooky girl bat has been left hanging in the park.

"She forgot to lock the garage today," Rico says as we turn down Vaughan Road.

"What? Who?"

"My neighbor. I can get my stuff. You got a bag or something?"

"No," I say. "What do we need a bag for?"

"Never mind. I bet she has one in the garage somewhere. In my house there's no such thing as privacy. I have to share a room with my older brother. He's always blabbing on the phone with girls. It's pathetic. If you go in the living room, my sister's there with my mother and my aunt and you can't even watch TV because they tell you to turn it down all the time so you can't even hear what you're trying to watch.

"And Mom goes through my room," Rico goes on. "Right while I'm standing there, she goes through my room. Can't even take a dump without someone knocking on the door asking what's taking so long. Do you have any brothers or sisters?"

I've known Rico for, like, five years. He's a grade ahead of me, so we don't hang out much. Still, I can't believe he doesn't remember anything I tell him.

"I have a cousin, but she doesn't live with us. And I don't have any pets and my mother doesn't go through my room. I can't remember the last time my mother even opened my door. We have two bathrooms and I could take all day to take a dump if I wanted. I could shit my heart out." Rico looks at me like I exist for a second. I don't think he's ever heard me swear before.

I swear sometimes. A lot of guys swear just to look tough and stuff. I like how Lucy called Rico a Moran. Now that was a good put-down. He didn't even know what hit him. I *will* swear when I want to, though.

We go down the alley behind Rico's house. He locks his bike to the back fence and motions for me to duck down. Nobody is around, but I do it anyway. We get to his neighbor's garage and sure enough it's not fully locked.

Rico lifts the door slowly. It sounds like a screaming kitten as it opens up. It squeaks so loud I can't help laughing at the look on Rico's face. He looks like the cops are going to spring out of the bushes and shoot him for opening a garage door. He won't lift it any higher. He shoos me in under this half-foot crack under the door.

It smells cold in here. It feels like being in a cave. I think of Lucy again and look up at the ceiling. A canoe is balanced over the rafters.

This would be better if Tom were here. He'd probably smack his hand against the canoe and knock it down.

Rico squirms on his belly like a trapped bug trying to get through the opening. He grunts and gasps. His butt won't fit under the door.

"Help me, idiot," he says. So I lean over and open the door more. It makes a huge squeaking sound, like nails on the blackboard. "Not like that, stupid." He gets in and pushes me into a corner and puts his hand over my mouth. We stand like that for at least a couple of minutes. You'd think it was diamonds he had in here. I want to bite his hand, but I remember: brown bats don't draw blood.

Finally, he takes his hand off. "That was a close call," he says. He goes to the corner of the garage and puts his hand down a pipe. He pulls out a pack of cigarettes, some matches and a couple of magazines. Playboys. Oh, brother.

"Do you see a plastic bag?" he says. I look around, but I hope I don't find one. He wants to transport his stash to some other hiding spot. I'm here to help pull off the heist and stow the goods.

"Here." He's found a ratty old garbage bag that might even have had a dead animal in it at some point. He puts the stuff in it and shoves it at me. "Come on, let's go." I hesitate for a moment. He's already under the door. "Come on. You want to get caught?" No, I don't want to get caught.

If I am good, it's because being bad is such a hassle. You've got to worry about getting caught and you've got to hide things. It takes a lot of energy. Besides, there are way better ways to get in trouble than smoking and looking at dirty magazines. I could be getting in trouble for trying to fly midgets off kites like Moran. Now, there's something worth getting caught for.

"Where are we going?" I ask.

"Your place. Come on."

Perfect. That's exactly what I need.

If Tom was here, he'd know what to say. What am I thinking? If Tom was here, we'd be halfway to my place already. He'd race us back for cigarettes and naked women.

I roll under the door with the garbage bag. Rico slams the door shut and whips down the alley. I have to run again. You hardly ever have to run when you aren't being bad.

I hope Elys isn't home.

"Elys?" I call out. The house is empty.

"Wow, that is a big TV set. You get cable?"

It figures that Rico would be interested in the television. Now it's going to take me forever to get him upstairs so that he can show me the dirty magazines, give me a cigarette and leave. I want to get the whole thing over with before Elys shows up.

He plunks himself down on the couch and grabs the remote.

What would Tom do? What would Lucy do? What would I do if I were someone else?

I walk over, take the remote from his hand and say, "Do you want to smoke or don't you?"

Rico follows me upstairs to my room. When we get there we open the garbage bag, pull out the mags and smokes and light up. We kneel by the window to blow the smoke outside and use my green plastic Viper Station as an ashtray.

The smoke itches my throat. It's like sucking warm dust. I want to cough, but I swallow instead. I won't give Rico the satisfaction. His cigarette smoke keeps getting in my eyes.

"You ever smoke before?" he asks me.

"Only second-hand," I say.

Rico nods. "You're a smoking virgin. I just ruined you for life. You're addicted now, Ter. There's no turning back." He grins so wide he loses his eyes.

Rico puts out his butt in my Viper Station. The plastic melts. He opens one of the magazines and starts flipping through.

"I found these under my brother's mattress. He's too embarrassed to say anything about them missing. I mean, what's he going to do, tell Mom? Ha." He passes one to me. I go through it slowly. Fortunately there are a lot of pages with words on them. I want to see a naked woman, but I don't want to see a naked woman.

I've seen my mom naked a few times accidentally. It wasn't that interesting. It was kind of like seeing a baby naked. You just can't think of your mother as a woman that way. Other women, you just can't help but want to see them naked. I try not to think about it too much.

I watch Rico look at the centerfold. He's slouched against my wall and he has another cigarette in his mouth. I can't see his face. I can only see this naked lady with huge tanned boobs and shiny lipstick on puckered lips on the back of the page he's looking at. She's upside-down.

I think about being a bat. Bats are mammals so they must have sex. I wonder if they do it upside-down or flying? I think about bats doing it while flying.

Maybe I am interested in the magazines, but there's no way I'm looking at them with Rico here. I

51

don't think it's respectful to look at naked women when someone else is in the room. It's just not right. Rico did this to me. I can't help looking at that upside-down naked woman and thinking about bats doing it while flying.

I reach for another cigarette to make like I'm more interested in smoking than I am in naked women. I just sit there and smoke and it feels like my lungs are filling with car exhaust. My eyes are leaking. My mouth is pasty. I still can't stop thinking about bats doing it in mid-air. Then my mind changes the bats into naked women with wings and it just keeps getting stupider.

I'm trying to shake it out of my head when Rico looks up. He's got this startled look on his face.

"What time is it?" he asks and looks at my digital clock, which reads 2:41. "I gotta go, Ter." He stands up and makes for my door. I haven't finished my cigarette yet.

He opens the door and Elys is standing right there. I whip the smoke behind my back, but I'm choking so hard trying to hold in the smoke that I start coughing and it blows out my mouth and my nose at the same time.

Elys is laughing.

"Gotta go, Ter," Rico mutters and runs past Elys. She's seen me with the smoke already, not to mention the dirty magazine on my lap.

"Well, well, well," Elys says. She walks in and takes the magazine from my lap. She lifts it up and lets the centerfold fall loose. "Hello, Miss March. Why, Miss March, what nice tan lines you have." She turns it toward me and points at the picture. "Get a load of this." As if I could do anything but stare at Miss March when she's four inches in front of my face.

"Airbrush city," says Elys. I take another puff from the cigarette. She takes it out of my hand and walks to the bathroom with it. I hear the toilet flush. While she's in there, I stuff the magazines back in the garbage bag and hustle them under my mattress. She comes back in, scans the room and then sits beside me on the bed.

"You get away with this once," she says. "Once, okay? I catch you smoking ever again, I rat to your mom. And I'll tell her about the girlie magazines." She pokes the mattress beside her to let me know she's on to me. She has my number big time. Man, oh, man. She puts her arms around my shoulders. I wish like hell I'd stayed in the park this morning.

"I understand about you wanting to look at naked women, but I wish you would wait until you can see real ones."

What is she talking about?

"I can see real ones?" I sputter. Elys guffaws in that smug, know-it-all way of hers.

"Yeah. In your future. Those magazine women aren't real. I mean, they're real, but…" I'm not getting her. They sure look real to me. Real naked. All smooth, tall and tanned with long hair and big lips. They look like real good women to me.

"I mean," Elys says more firmly now, "you shouldn't be able to buy women the way you buy — I don't know — ketchup. You don't buy women off the magazine rack. Besides, those magazines are false advertising. You'll never date a woman who looks like that."

Now I'm insulted.

"How do you know?" I say.

"Any woman good enough to date you is going to be way more beautiful than any of those Playboy bunnies and you'll know it whether your eyes are open or closed."

I roll my eyes. Elys whips her arm off my shoulder, pulls the mattress up and gets the garbage bag. She pulls the magazines out and opens them.

"They are bottles of ketchup. They are commodities. How would you like to get paid for taking your clothes off? How would that make you feel about yourself? What if you weren't good-looking enough to take your clothes off for money? How would you like to be treated like you were only valuable because of what you looked like? Because you were a certain height, or a certain weight, or your eyes were a certain color?"

I think about Moran's airborne midgets and the Midget Employment Stabilization Board. Then I think "Naked Women Employment Stabilization Board," and how there is way more employment for naked women than there is for midgets. I mean, small people.

"It's not funny to be funny looking," I say, remembering Lucy's words. Elys looks at me like I'm whacko. I don't think I've ever seen her so angry. She doesn't seem angry at me. It's the magazines she is angry about — those naked women and a world full of Morans.

7

Mom and Farley are supposed to be going away this weekend. I have to play goody-good little good boy for Farley on Friday. Mom tells me this over dinner. Hot dogs. I put a ton of ketchup on mine. It is a secret joke with myself. Mom should notice. Usually I only have mustard.

I don't even like ketchup that much. I don't think you should put sweet stuff on meat — even pretend meat like hot dogs. Think of sprinkling sugar on steak if you don't believe me.

*

I get to the park and I'm looking for Rico so that I can call him a Moran. He is in big trouble for taking off so fast yesterday.

Nobody's here except Boobacious.

"Have you seen Rico?" I ask her. I just want information. I don't want a discussion. I don't want anything to slip out accidentally.

"Did you touch Lucy yesterday?" she asks. Man, oh, man, I'm in trouble. Lucy must've busted her head open or something.

"Why? I didn't hit her. Bats don't hit." I know I'm blushing.

"What?" Boobacious asks.

"Her head touched my shoe. I swear, I didn't do anything."

"Did your hands touch her head?" she asks. Now it's my turn to be confused.

"What?"

"I had to send Lucy home because she had head lice. Now, is there any way you could have it?"

"Lice?" I want to itch my head bad, but I can't because Boobacious will think I have lice. Just thinking about lice makes my head itchy.

"I don't have lice," I tell her.

"That's not what I asked, Terence." How does she know my name? I should know hers. Her real one, I mean. "All I'm asking is did you touch her in any way that you could get lice?" I wonder if lice can climb into your sneakers and crawl up into your hair. I just had the most horrible thought about where lice could go in a body.

"I didn't touch anything, I swear to God."

"Are you sure?" It's like she's trying to get me to confess to some kind of crime, or, worse, maybe she thinks me and Lucy are going around. We might be bats, but it's not like that. Adults think everything is about sex or money.

"Look, she's not my girlfriend, if that's what you mean. I didn't touch her. I don't have lice."

She looks at my head like she wants to touch it. I want to cover my head with my arms.

57

Rico's coming down the path toward us. He's got his hands in his pockets. One day he's going to fall right on his big round head.

"I took cootie girl home," Rico says, like he's expecting some reward. I give him the evilest eye I have and he looks at me like he's all innocent.

"Where'd you go yesterday, Moran?" I say. Boobacious takes a walk around the wading pool.

"What are you talking about, dickhead?"

"I'm talking about you running home. I had to take the heat for both of us. Those weren't even my magazines. And my Viper Station is ruined. It's all melted." I never get to say this much in a fight. If Tom were here I wouldn't get to say anything. I'm so angry, but it's not even about the Viper Station or the magazines. I hate Rico today. I can't even look at his face.

"I didn't see the point of me sticking around. What was she going to do? Yell at some stranger? You said you wanted to smoke."

"I did not." He practically made me do it. "It was all you, Rico. You pushed me into it. You think you're Mr. Big Man pushing everyone around. You nearly killed Lucy yesterday."

"You're crazy. She was hanging upside-down already. Maybe she was trying to get the cooties to fall off her head."

I am so mad, I can hardly see. I want to beat on

him, but he's, like, a foot taller than I am. And bats don't hit.

I can't stand to look at his face for one more second. I run out of the park.

I bet he didn't even check to see if Daphne or Lucy's parents were home. What is she supposed to do all day. Sit at home and have lice?

This car honks at me when I cross Bathurst Street. I give him the finger. Anyway, they should put a crosswalk here. Lots of little kids in this neighborhood want to go to the park.

I get to Lucy's apartment building, but I can't find the front door. I have to look all through the mall on the bottom floor. Finally, I find the apartment part of the building. I don't know Lucy's last name so I can't buzz up.

How can you be friends with someone and not know her last name? I'm looking down the list of last names to see if any of them ring a bell, when Russell the chess guy/pervert comes in.

"Hello," he says. I think he recognizes me. I want to ask him Lucy's last name, but I don't want to tell him about the lice, so I end up not saying anything. He holds the door open for me and I follow him in. He obviously thinks I know where I'm going.

"You going to Lucy's?"

I nod. He pushes the button for the elevator. He is carrying a grocery bag. It has corn chips and Coke in it. I didn't know guys his age ate junk food.

He sees me looking at his groceries and says, "Do you play chess?"

"No. I don't know how. I play Scrabble with my cousin sometimes." The elevator comes and I get on with him. I think about Rico saying Russell's a pervert, and I make my way to the corner of the elevator. Maybe he uses the junk food to lure kids up to his apartment.

Russell pushes two buttons. I guess one of them is for Lucy's floor. I try to look interested in the floor numbers as they light up above the door.

"I could teach you to play chess, if you liked," he says. Does he mean now? In his house? "At the park, I mean," he adds, like he can read my mind. I can't believe Rico, man. He doesn't know anything. Just because a guy hangs out in a park doesn't make him a pervert. Then again...

"Lucy said it's easy. She said she'd show me how," I say. The doors open. I wait for Russell to get off. He looks at me.

"Well?" he says. I figure this is Lucy's floor and I step off. "She's a good teacher," Russell says as the doors close.

I don't like big apartment buildings. The halls always remind me of those cartoon hallways where all the characters run in and out of apartments. I hate those cartoons. I wonder about all the characters who live in those apartments they are running through.

They ignore so much on television. It's like the camera decides what's important and it's always the same stuff. It's so predictable, it's sickening. Plus, there's always a happy ending which is just a lie. I can't remember the last happy ending in my life. I can't remember ever feeling like everything was going to be A-okay forever starting now. It's all a big lie. It doesn't work like that in real life. Real life is full of all these boring extra times and stupid little stuff like picking your nose and doing laundry.

I walk up and down the hall looking at the doors. I don't know what I expect — maybe a big bat symbol on the door, or a big arrow sign that says, "Lice here." I am tempted to put my ear against the doors to listen for Lucy's voice.

If Tom were here he might just knock on all the doors and ask for Lucy. Only Tom wouldn't look for Lucy. I bet Tom has a flat head from carrying canoes around. Tom, Mr. Big Mouth with a flat head. I guess I miss him.

I hear the elevator doors opening. I run for the door to the stairs. I don't want anyone to call the cops on me for loitering in apartment hallways. I peek through the door to watch whoever it is come down the hall.

It's Lucy. She's walking down the hall fidgeting

61

with something behind her back. I don't know whether to stay hidden or not. What if she sees me hiding? I'd look like the world's biggest jerk.

I fling open the door and say "Hi," way too loudly. Lucy drops something on the floor and screams. I want to disappear back into the stairwell. Instead, I run up and reach down for the bottle of shampoo she dropped. The top opened and it's oozing all over the place. Lucy has her hand on her throat.

"I'm sorry. I didn't mean to scare you." I put the lid back on the shampoo. I've got the stuff all over my hands. It smells like soapy green apples. Lucy grabs the bottle from my hands and marches down the hall.

"I'm sorry," I say again and follow her.

"What are you doing here?" she asks as we stop at her door. Like me, she has to retrieve a hide-a-key to get inside.

"I didn't know which apartment was yours," I say. She stares at me like she's waiting for more of an answer. It's like she can't hear you unless you're telling the truth. It must be a bat thing. "I think I'm a bat," I tell her. "Bats help other bats, right?" I can't look her in the eye, so I look down at the pool of shampoo spreading down the hall. She turns around, opens the door and walks in.

"Well?" she says. I walk in to a total pigsty. I thought I was messy, but this place…man, oh, man.

So many newspapers on the floor that it looks like they were trying to carpet the place with them. Dirty glasses and dishes, some with old food still on them, are all over the end tables and the coffee table. The couch is draped in sat-on clothes on top of a wrinkled sheet. Underneath, it looks like a decent couch.

I walk over to the window. I see Lake Ontario. I see all the high-rises downtown. I see the CN Tower.

"Awesome view," I shout to Lucy. It's the one nice thing I can think of to say.

"Be quiet," she says. She points to the bedroom. Her dad must be asleep. She sits cross-legged on top of all the stuff on the couch. She still has her bat-cape on. Today she has little teardrops painted on her face. You can still see the squiggles from yesterday underneath. You'd think anyone used to washing her face that hard would think to do her hair, too.

"Stop looking at me," she says.

"Sorry," I say. I look away. I stand up and look out the window some more. I think I can see the top of Mom's office building. I wonder if she is in conference with Farley right now, planning some big weekend fun. I bet she leaves Elys a lot of money. I can probably convince Elys to take me to the Science Centre. Lucy, too. We could yell our heads off in the soundproof hallway, or do those inkblot tests for the mind. I bet Lucy would see bats in every one of them.

I turn to ask her.

"Don't look at me!" she yells. She has her hands over her eyes. Her cape shudders. She looks up toward the hall and covers her mouth. I go and sit beside her. The only thing I know to do is pat her on the back. She jerks away at first, but then she lets me. We stay like that for a while. The room smells like wet pizza and apple juice. She sniffs a few times, but she doesn't sob.

"I'm not a freak, you know," she says.

"I know."

"I don't know what to do," she says and starts crying. She stuffs the end of her bat cape in her mouth to keep from making noise. I pat her back some more. I can see tears dropping on her leg and bouncing onto her sneakers.

I go to get her a glass of water.

The kitchen is even messier than the living room. The dishes are all over the place and the garbage is overflowing. On the counter is an old cheese wrapper with some fuzzy vegetable on it. I think it is a zucchini, but it could just as easily be a cucumber, or even a carrot. Only the cupboards are clean — empty of all the dishes. I look on the kitchen table for a glass to wash and see a stack of notes, all written on toilet paper.

"Michael: do dishes," one says. At the bottom in different handwriting is, "Lorraine: buy bread."

Michael and Lorraine must be Lucy's parents. Another one says, "Michael: pay phone bill," and at the bottom, again, in different handwriting, is, "Lorraine: clean bathtub."

There are, like, twenty of these pieces of toilet paper stacked on the table. Someone has blown his or her nose in a couple of them — you can still see the magic marker writing on the sides.

On the corner of the kitchen table is a glass full of colored magic markers. They all have their caps on. Lucy must take care of the markers to keep them fresh for making her tattoos — or maybe to keep them fresh so that her parents can write these notes to one another. I guess with her father working nights and her mom I-don't-know-where during the days, they don't have much time for housework — only enough time for writing notes on toilet paper. Or maybe this is how they have a fight.

I wash out a glass, fill it with water and take it to Lucy. She takes a sip. She blows her nose into her bat cape. Gross. She gulps down half of the water. She puts the glass on the floor and sighs.

"I don't know what to do," she says to the air. I can almost see the words float out of her mouth.

"Maybe you should wash your hair," I say. She slices me with her laser eyes. I ignore her and pick up the shampoo.

"I stole it," she says. I can't believe it. "My sister

65

Daphne has shampoo, but she's got a lock on her door so I can't get in. My mom showers at the gym at the university and there's a shower where my dad works, because it's so hot with the ovens and everything. Anyway, there's no shampoo in the bathroom. I was using dish soap and then just soap. Daphne's mad at Mom so she hasn't bought any groceries in two weeks. She's supposed to look out for me, but she's been getting extra hours at work. I think she spent the money on new shoes. She gave me $10 last week, but I spent it already." She chokes it out. "I bought too many egg rolls. I didn't know shampoo was so expensive."

"I get $10 for allowance every week," I say. "It's hardly enough for ice creams and Slurpies."

"You must be rich," Lucy says.

"I don't think we are," I say. But I'm not so sure. "We have a pretty big TV set and I get new clothes twice a year."

"That's rich," she says. "We used to be rich before we moved here. Dad says it's because Toronto is really pricy. I think we have enough money. It's just that nobody has time to buy anything. He's working. Mom's cramming all these courses in so she can get a better job. And they are mad at each other all the time now because they hate it here. They don't even want to live here. They won't even talk to one another. It's all my fault." How can it be her fault? "It was going okay until Daphne got the job a couple of months ago. Now she doesn't have any time to shop or do laundry or anything and my parents are so stubborn. Mom thinks Dad has more time and Dad thinks Mom has more time and they have both been in a bad mood for a month. I mean, I would buy the stuff if they gave the money to me. I'm old enough to take care of myself. I don't see why Daphne should have to do everything." I look around at the living-room mess.

"I don't think there's any law against you cleaning up," I say.

"But I'm only twelve," she says and smiles at me, bat-style — with her mouth open and all her teeth showing.

That starts me laughing, and then she starts laughing and then she puts a sweater or something over my face to shut me up because her dad is sleeping, and we're both laughing and biting down on clothing. Lucy falls back into the couch, she's laughing so hard, and we both hear her bat cape rip. We both stop laughing for a second and look at each other while we listen for sounds of her dad. She puts her head against the wall, then so do I. We can both hear him snoring and that starts us laughing all over again. Lucy falls on the floor holding her stomach. The newspapers rustle under her and make it sound like it's raining inside.

I get on the floor and start to roll Lucy up in the newspapers. It's like she is a big fish and I'm packing her up for dinner. She squirms, but I get one end folded over her feet. I go to do the same to the head end, to pack her up real good. She sits straight up, her arms still wrapped in newspaper. Her face has a fierce look of warning on it.

The lice — she doesn't want me to touch her head.

That's the end of the fun. She stands up and the papers fall around her feet.

I pick up the newspapers and put them in a pile. I keep picking up papers until all the papers are in one big pile. Then I start taking all the dishes into the kitchen. On my third trip back to pick up more dishes, I run into Lucy in the doorway. She cracks me a shy smile, but we don't say anything.

Once all the dishes are in the kitchen, Lucy starts filling up the sink with water. I fold the clothes on the couch and put them in a pile underneath the coffee table. By the time I get back to the kitchen, Lucy is up to her elbows in bubbles.

"I thought you didn't have any dish detergent?" I whisper. Lucy points to the bottle of shampoo by the sink and we both break out in giggles again. Lucy puts the dishes into the water carefully, so they don't make too much noise. I use Lucy's bat cape to dry the glasses. By the time they are done, the whole thing is soaked. We still have the dishes and pots to do. Lucy takes the cape off for the first time ever and hands it to me.

I don't feel right using it anymore, now that it's not on her. It's like she handed me her leg or something. Lucy looks naked without her cape on. She looks a lot smaller.

I half wish we hadn't started with the dishes. Tom would have a fit if he ever found out I helped a girl do dishes and even had fun doing it. If Tom found out, I'd never hear the end of it.

Lucy won't tell. Bats don't tell on other bats. I don't know if there's an actual bat rule book, but that sounds right to me.

Lucy has to refill the sink three times before we are even near finished. We decide to let a few of the pots soak. I watch Lucy wipe the counters. She lifts the toilet-paper notes up and puts them back down again. They are the only thing left on the kitchen table — well, them and the glass full of markers. We do a really good job.

The place looks seven thousand percent better. We could vacuum the living room, but Lucy's dad is still asleep. I swear, I forgot he was there for a while.

"Terence," Lucy says as we are admiring our cleaning job, "will you help me with my hair?" She asks me in a whisper.

I don't know if I want to put my hands in lice hair.

Then again, it can't be any worse than the rest of the mess we just cleared out. Bats help bats.

I nod and Lucy holds up her finger and leaves the room.

She comes back wearing a brown bathing suit. It's the bathing suit that reminds me that she's a girl. It's easier to remember Lucy is a bat than it is to remember she's a girl. The bathing suit's a little small for her, so the neck is pulled down lower than it should go. I can see she's growing boobs. I look up at her face real quick. I can't be treating a bat like she's ketchup.

We go into the bathroom. Lucy locks the door. She kneels on the bathmat and turns the water on. Only one of the bulbs in the light is working.

"Help me make sure I get it all out," she says. She leans over the tub and wets her hair under the faucet. I sit on the toilet to watch. She lathers up. Her eyes are shut tight to stop soap from getting in them.

I can't help stealing a longer look at her skinny body. She has fuzzy blonde hairs growing on her upper back. You can hardly tell they're there at all.

She sticks her hair back under the faucet and washes the soap out. I can see some lice in the soap. They look like tiny crabs. Their little bodies circle around the drain like pieces of wet rice.

"Can you check my head?" Lucy asks. She keeps her head over the bathtub. I go over and kneel beside her on the bathmat. I'm not sure exactly what to do. I lean over her and take pieces of her hair and look at them. I don't see anything. I put my hand on the back of her neck. It is soft. I part her hair at the top and look at the scalp. I see a little wriggling piece of something. I take a quick breath and slowly take my hands off her.

"I saw one," I say. "You better try again." She hits the side of the tub really hard and kicks her foot against the floor. "I'm sure one more time will do it, Lucy."

"It better do it. I don't know. Maybe you need special shampoo. Get out, GET OUT!" she yells as she lathers up again. I look at the back of her neck. I'll get to put my hand there again.

There's a knock on the door. Lucy's head is under the faucet, so she doesn't hear. I kick her foot. She turns.

"What?" She hears the next knock.

"Lucy?" It's her dad.

"Yeah?"

"I told you, no friends allowed during the day." He sounds tired and pissed off. Just like Elys before her morning coffee. "Who's in there with you?"

Lucy and I look at each other. It's like we both suddenly realize that we aren't the same sex. Adults wouldn't understand about us both being bats.

"It's only Terry, Dad," Lucy says.

I don't let people call me Terry because it sounds like a girl's name. I am always Terence. Only I don't mind so much if it saves my butt.

We both listen and wait for her dad to leave the door.

"Hurry up, okay?" he says finally, and we hear the floor squeak. I breathe a huge sigh of relief. But Lucy still looks pretty nervous.

"You've got to get out of here fast when I open the door. Go straight into the closet across the hall, okay?" I nod. She wraps her head in a towel and listens at the door. After a few seconds she looks at me and then opens it. I fly across the hall and open the closet door. It has a bunch of shelves in it, but I can fit under the bottom one.

A roll of toilet paper falls on me. I hold it next to my chest to keep it quiet. Sure enough I hear Lucy's dad coming down the hall.

"What were you doing in there?" he asks.

"Washing my hair."

"In your bathing suit?" Lucy must be nodding. He doesn't sound angry anymore, just curious. "Where'd your friend go?"

"Gone," Lucy says. I hear the washroom door close and knock my head against a shelf. I put my hand over my mouth to keep from yelping. I bite down on the roll of toilet paper in case I forget to keep my mouth shut. There's a boxing match going on in my chest. I wonder if Lucy can hear it through the door.

I press my ear against it and fall over into the hall.

Lucy's father is staring down at me, and I've got that roll of toilet paper stuck in my mouth. Lucy is right behind him looking petrified. Her arms are shaking. She needs to eat more.

"What the hell is going on?" Lucy's dad booms. He's wearing a bathrobe. People always look meaner when they are angry in their bathrobes. He's got spiky red hair just like Lucy. It's sticking up all over the place like a crazy man's.

I close my eyes, hoping it will all go away.

"Get up," he says. So I do. I take the toilet paper out of my mouth and put it on the shelf in the closet. All the time I can feel him watching my every move.

"Are you Terry?"

I nod. He has his hands on my shoulders so I can't run away. I want to say, "I'm just a kid, I'm just a kid," but I can't help thinking about those ketchup magazines I've got hidden under my mattress.

Lucy's dad is looking me straight in the eye, and I'm having a hard time looking innocent.

"Terence was just helping me clean up," Lucy says. Her dad looks her over, too, takes in her wet hair and her bathing suit, and my dry hair and dry clothes. Lucy backs into the living room. "See, Dad?"

He grabs the back of my collar and pulls me with him into the living room. Right away he softens up. He moves his hand to my head.

"Okay," he says. He doesn't look particularly happy. He looks like he just ran five miles in his bathrobe. "But I told you no friends, Lucy. I'm going to have to ask you to leave, Terry." I wince a little at him saying my name like that. I feel my heart pounding harder in my chest. I don't want to leave Lucy alone to get in trouble. Not like Rico left me.

"I'll see you tomorrow, Terence," Lucy says. "I have an idea I want to talk to you about."

"Like what?" her dad says.

"Daaaad," Lucy says. She's trying to smooth it over and it's working a bit. "It's kid's stuff, Dad." She puts her hand on his arm. "You wouldn't understand." Her dad takes another look at the living room. He nods and rubs his eyes. He looks like he hasn't slept in twenty years. He walks back toward the washroom.

Lucy walks me to the door.

"Thanks, Terence," she says. "Meet me at the picnic table tomorrow." She closes the door. Instead of taking the elevator, I run down all the stairs. I run ten floors in two minutes.

*

When I get home, this weenie guy in an orange tie is reading the comics on the couch. He has his shoes off. He's wearing gym socks with a suit. Elys would have something to say about that. She may not have a job, but she knows a thing or two about what's wrong in work attire, and gym socks top the list.

I'm thinking, "Make yourself at home, buddy." I'm thinking it, but what I say is, "Uh, hi."

The guy pops right up, like I'm his captain. He has one of those moustaches where the ends grow down around the mouth like two daggers. It makes his head look bigger, somehow. It's the wrong kind of moustache for someone in a suit. My mom likes guys who look like they should be wearing motorcycle outfits but are wearing suits instead.

"You must be Terence," he says, sticking out his hand. I have to take it. "I'm Farley. Your mom's upstairs." As if I didn't know. "You're off school now, right?"

"Right," I say. I sit down on the rocking chair. Farley's in my usual spot. I don't know what I thought he would look like, but he's shorter than that.

The guy looks me over. He seems to be looking for something to ask me about. I would ask him something, but I don't feel like it right now.

"You've got your mother's eyes," he says.

I think, "Better than having her boobs," but what I say is, "Yeah, I guess. We both have 20/20 vision."

Farley laughs.

I can tell by the way he's looking at me that he has it bad for my mom. I can just tell. He looks happy about me, which is the wrong way for a boyfriend to act about his girlfriend's kid. He's supposed to look more scared.

I close my eyes because Farley is looking at them all goofy.

"You been out bothering the girls, Ter?" he says. He shouldn't call me Ter right off. That's a mistake. "You look plum tuckered." Now I have to open my eyes again.

"Yeah, I was washing my girlfriend's hair and boy, are my hands tired," I say. What do I care what he thinks. I usually don't talk back to adults.

I think Farley appreciates my honesty, though, because he's nodding.

"I never wash hair before the third date," he says. "What's she like, your girlfriend?"

"She's a bat," I say. He is definitely going to be telling Mom about our little conversation here. It will give her something to chew on while Farley's trying to impress her with his bad French in Montreal. He raises his furry eyebrows. "She hangs upside-down from a noose in the attic." Sometimes it doesn't matter what you say.

"Oh," he says. Lucky for him, Mom comes downstairs. She's got on her weekend clothes — black shorts and T-shirt.

"Terence. Good. I'm glad you're home, hon."

"You said to be here for when you left."

"Yes. And here you are." Now she's the one acting all goofy. She sounds like somebody's mom, but not mine. She's talking to me but looking at Farley. She doesn't ever call me hon. She calls me "Ter, you whacko, be a sweet thing and get your mom a sandwich." Sometimes she calls me Ter Bear, usually after a particularly bad day at work, or once when I got a big splinter and she had to pick it out with a sterilized needle. "So, you met Farley?"

"Yeah. I did." Now I totally regret saying anything to the guy about anything. He winks at me. Yeesh.

"Terence was telling me about this bat he knows."

"A bat?" Mom smiles, like my whole life is a joke.

"Yeah. He says she likes to hang upside-down in attics."

"I hope you aren't going into strange houses, hon," Mom says. She's not getting it at all. Neither is he. Anyway, I can tell by the way they're looking at each other that I could say that the CN Tower toppled over and they would say, "That's nice," and go to Montreal.

What I end up saying is, "No. I just know this bat. That's all." I start rocking the chair and close my eyes again.

"You got everything?" Farley asks.

I wonder if my father had a moustache like Farley's. Maybe Elys knows. Mom tells her a lot of stuff. Mom says she didn't know my father very well. She says she loves him for giving her the best gift ever: me.

It felt strange being in a house with a father today. I always feel like I have to be really careful when a father is around. They seem more naturally mean than mothers. Mom lets me do anything I want — as long as it doesn't mean any work for her.

"Can I go to the Science Centre this weekend, Mom?" It's the perfect time to ask. Farley's got her bag slung over his shoulder and is making for the door. I can tell he doesn't know whether to stop or not.

"I'll be there in a sec, hon," Mom says to him. What's with this hon thing? She fiddles in her purse, pulls out some cash and puts it on the coffee table.

"Here. Tell Elys I said it was okay, but only if she's up to it. She has a life, too, you know, sweetie. I'll be back Sunday night. If she doesn't take you we'll go out for pizza or something, okay?" I nod. She takes another hard long look at me. "You all right, Ter? You look tired. I hope you haven't been prowling in strange houses. Where's this attic?" She strokes my hair. I'm too old for that. I pull my head away.

"There is no attic, Mom."

"Was it in a movie?"

"It's too hard to explain," I say. Let her figure out a gap for a change.

"I want to hear all about it on Sunday. I have to get going now. It's seven hours to Montreal and I'm driving."

"Can't Farley drive?"

"He doesn't have a car, hon." She makes her way to the door.

"Mom." She turns around for a second. I was going to tell her not to call me hon, but she's got this huge smile on her face that I just can't wreck.

"Bye, Ter Bear," she says. "Have a good time. I love you."

"You, too." She closes the door.

8

I don't want to wake Elys up, but I told Lucy I'd meet her at the picnic table and Elys is supposed to take us to the Science Centre today. At least, she said she would. So I have to wake her up but I don't know how.

I try making a lot of noise downstairs. I make some coffee. I don't know how anyone could drink that stuff. It tastes like mudwater that's had dandelions soaking in it. I bang the pot on the table a few times and listen for movement.

The noise doesn't work, so I make some toast and take it up on a tray with the coffee. Elys is cranky in the mornings. She won't even let me talk to her before her coffee when she stays over. She doesn't get up until after 11:00 a lot of the time, too. She says there's no real point. She used to get up 7:30 every day her first few months out of school. She'd look for work all day long. Now she says it doesn't take all day to not find work. Now she says it takes exactly twelve hours a week to not find a job.

Even walking in the room doesn't wake her up. I have to pry her eyes open with my fingers. Her eyes are open but I know she can't see me. It's like she's still dreaming. Very freaky. She swats my hand away and

gets this cross look on her face with those crazy eyes.
I pull back, but she goes right back to sleep. It's no use.

*

I go to the park to find Lucy by myself. Nobody's there but Russell and his chess board. You'd think there would be more people here on the weekend, but it doesn't work out that way.

Russell and I are the only two people in the park, so there's no way I can ignore him. I can tell he's trying not to look at me with those huge glasses of his. Anyway, Lucy said to meet her at the picnic table.

"Hi," I say to Russell. He nods. "Have you seen Lucy?"

"Not today. I was hoping she would come play some chess with me. It's early yet."

Early. That's why no one's here. Russell looks like he wants me to go away. But I have nowhere to go. I think about going to sit on the bench by the wading pool, but that seems stupid, so I sit down with Russell.

"Lucy told me to meet her here," I say. He nods. I didn't think perverts were shy. What does Rico know? Maybe Rico thinks a pervert is a guy who plays chess.

"So…you want me to show you how to play chess?" he asks. I shrug. I've got nothing better to do.

"Yes, please," I say. He smiles like he's never heard the word please before. He doesn't look like a pervert so much anymore. He looks more like an old bus driver.

Russell starts telling me all about how each of the pieces move. I keep looking over toward Lucy's apartment building and then over to where Rico would come from if he was going to show up.

Russell tells me about how the queen is the most powerful piece on the board, which kind of surprises me. You would think the king would have more power since he's the one all the other guys on the board are after, but it turns out the king can only move one square in any direction. I like the way the bishop moves in a diagonal. It's harder to think diagonally than straight up and down and across. Lucy was right about it not being so tough to figure out.

Russell sets us up to play a game. Remembering where all the pieces go is the hardest thing about chess. Russell says for me to go first because I'm red. Now I see how hard the game must be, because how do I know where to move anything?

I shove a pawn forward.

Tom would never play chess. Never in a millennium. He would definitely prefer to look at nudie ketchup pictures than play chess. I never thought I would ever do anything that Tom wouldn't do. I figure we're about even. He gets to learn about canoeing, and I get to learn about kites and chess. And about being a bat, but I probably won't tell him that.

At first it seems like nothing is happening in the game, and I can see how chess gets its boring reputation. But then I take one of Russell's pawns and he grabs my bishop without me even seeing it coming. I swear, I had my eyes peeled the whole time and I didn't see it at all.

The game becomes like the opposite of watching television. You have to be super aware of all these guys on the board at the same time, plus you have to think what Russell is going to do next. I can see why it has to be a quiet game.

I use my queen to cream his castle, which is threatening my knight. Then he takes her out with a knight, and my most powerful piece is gone.

"Man, oh, man," I say.

"You have to think three moves ahead," he says. I feel like telling him I'm only twelve, but it's a weenie thing to say.

He wins the first game and I ask if we can play again.

It's halfway through the third game and Russell has just taken my queen (again), when Elys shows up looking for me. I don't even see her. I just hear this whisper in my right ear. "Get his knight." And all of a sudden I see it. You can look at the board for hours and still not see everything going on there.

I take Russell's knight. He looks kind of pissed-off at Elys. I think he forgot he was playing a kid for a second.

I introduce them and Russell plays his bishop. I can't figure out why he did it. Maybe he's trying to throw me off the track. I can hear the two of them yammering away beside me, which is strange because neither of them are yammerers. It makes it hard to concentrate so I put my hands over my ears. I could take the bishop with my queen, but that's just what he wants me to do. Why? He's not in a position to take my queen...I don't think. Through my hands I hear Russell talking about his son's store. Something about special orders.

Then I see it. He wants me to move my queen because she is in a place dangerous to his king. I hear them talking about glasses and about both needing new prescriptions. I check out the board some more, then move my queen sideways and take out a pawn.

"Ha," I say. "Take that." Russell looks down at the board. I look over at Elys. She has this glint in her eye.

"Good," says Russell, then sighs. I got him. I really got him.

"Thanks for leaving breakfast on the bed for me, Ter," says Elys. "I rolled in the toast and had a dream about someone sandpapering my knee. Now the comforter has this huge coffee stain on it."

"No problem," I say. "Any time." I'm watching to see what move Russell will make. He's taking longer than usual.

"I thought you said you wanted to go to the Science Centre?" Elys says. I wish Russell would make his move. I want him to take my bishop so that I can get his queen. I wonder if he'll be able to figure it out. "Ter?"

"Huh?"

"Science Centre?" Elys asks.

"Uh. I thought Lucy would be here. It was really Lucy who wanted to go." Lucy doesn't know anything about the Science Centre. "I don't know where she is. I hope she's okay."

"Why wouldn't she be okay?" Russell asks. I don't want to tell them about the lice thing or her parents' toilet-paper notes, or the lock on her sister's door. Bats don't rat on bats.

"I don't know…Bathurst Street sure is busy. They should put a crosswalk there," I say and shake my head to try to convince them that I truly fear Lucy may have been run over just a block away. Like we wouldn't have heard the ambulance.

"Well, do you want to call her or what?" Elys asks. I wish Russell would take his turn.

"No. It wasn't really a firm plan. It was more just an idea. Maybe tomorrow?"

"You think you can just order up an outing any time you want? You think I'm a professional chaperon?" She sounds angry.

"No. That's not what I think," I say. Russell still

hasn't made his move. "What I think is that you have nothing better to do." I flash her a grin, but it goes down the wrong way. She stares me down with those black marble eyes of hers.

"That may be true, Terence, but I don't need to hear it from you." Elys gets up and leaves the table.

I didn't mean to hurt her feelings. I didn't even know I could hurt her feelings. She's heading toward Loblaws. I hope she gets one of those frozen lasagnas. I know Mom left her enough money. Lasagna is Tom's favorite. It's my favorite, too.

"Hey, Elys," I yell after her. She doesn't turn around. "Relax, it's the weekend." She stops in her tracks, lets her head fall forward and marches on. The weekend is, apparently, not good news for Elys. Someone should give her a job.

I pulled one over on Russell but he still wins the game. He shakes my hand this time.

"Good games, Terence. Come again." I can see he expects me to push off now, but I'm not ready to go.

"Do you think I could beat Lucy?" I ask.

"No," he says. I wait for an explanation but don't get one. I see Martin coming down the path. He's wearing shorts this time, and a white hat.

"Hey, it's that kid," he says, pointing at me. "Where's our favorite bat?" I shrug. I wish I could play another game. I should find Lucy and we could play bat to bat. "You'd better hang on to that one before she hangs on to you." Martin gnashes his teeth at me and makes little eep, eep noises.

"She's not a vampire," I tell him.

"That's what she tells you. But would a real vampire tell you she was a vampire? Think about that one. She seems awfully smart for a kid, don't you think?" Martin says.

"She would definitely beat you at chess," says Russell. He seems to loosen up when Martin's around. Just like I do when Tom is around, or Lucy, too, now I guess.

"Don't talk crazy talk," I say. They both laugh. Where is Lucy, anyway? It's got to be at least lunchtime. Maybe Daphne made her go to Fatso's. I hope so. She sure is scrawny. That book said bats have to eat all night just to keep up their weight.

Listen to me. I'm as bad as Lucy now. Must be a sign.

*

I find Elys at the Loblaws across the street. The air-conditioning is nice at first, but by aisle five I'm freezing. I pick out some smoothy peanut butter. Elys is always buying crunchy. I think she thinks the whole bits of peanuts are healthier than fully crushed ones.

I hit aisle six and see a bat scoping out the pasta section. I watch Lucy stuff a bag of linguini down the back of her shorts behind her cape.

"Lucy!" I holler. She looks around, sees me and gently finishes tucking the pasta in her waistband. I go up to her and whisper, "What are you doing?"

"What does it look like?" She moves down the aisle.

"It looks like you're stealing." I can hear how stupid I sound. Like, duh, you don't have to say it out loud. "Put it back. My cousin's here. My mom gave her some money. She'll get you some spaghetti."

"Do I look like a charity case?" She turns on her heel and heads down the aisle. I have to stop her.

"Yes," I scream. This old lady holding two cans of peaches gives me a sour look.

I race down the aisle. Lucy is leaving the store. I run after her. I bolt through the doors and two seconds later feel this hand on the back of my neck.

"Where do you think you're going?" the security guy says.

It's only then I realize I still have the peanut butter in my hand.

What a totally stunned move. I stole something without even meaning to. My heart is going faster than the speed of light.

"I…" I see Lucy up the street. She's turned around, but is making like she doesn't know me. She's looking past me, pretending to be looking for someone else.

"You'd better come with me," the guy says. I try to

give the peanut butter to him, but he just shakes his head. He's still got me by the neck. His hand is the size of a baseball glove. He doesn't seem particularly angry or anything. More like a guy who's just caught a fish. He's leading me down to the office past all the cashiers. They look at me, then at each other and make sucking noises with their teeth.

I feel like crying, but I hold the tears back. I'm sure bats don't cry in public. Now Mom is going to find out and she's not going to leave me with Elys anymore on the weekend and I'll never get to go to the Science Centre with Lucy. I might even have to go to jail or pay a fine.

I wish the guy would take his hand off my neck. He can trust me that far. I want to talk him out of taking me to the office. If I was going to steal something, it wouldn't be peanut butter. I'd steal chocolate bars maybe, or chips.

"Terence, there you are."

I've never been so glad to see Elys in all my life. She looks at me and then at the guy and then at the peanut butter in my hand, and then back at the guy again. She adjusts her glasses, clears her throat and takes the peanut butter from me.

"Great, you found it. Thanks, Ter Bear." She never calls me that. "Now, I need you to find the paper towels for me." I try to wriggle out of the guy's hand, but he tightens his grip.

"I just found this young man leaving the premises with an unpaid item." Security guys think they're so cool. I look down at the floor to avoid looking in Elys's eyes.

"Terence! I know I'm having trouble seeing, but I think I have it together enough to stay indoors." What is she on about? I look up at her and she's adjusting her glasses again and squinting.

"I know, but…"

"But nothing. That was a pretty stupid thing for you to do. You know they consider it stealing the second you leave the store."

"But I only…"

"Officer," (I love the way she calls him officer) "my cousin here is helping me do my shopping. I broke my new glasses the other day and I'm wearing my old ones, so I'm blind as a bat. I can't see a thing, and they cut into the side of my head in the most painful way so I've got a migraine to boot. Terence must have been looking for me. I'm afraid I've had a few little accidents today already."

"Like banging into that telephone pole," I say. The guy's dropped his hand and I feel so close to free, I can't resist teasing Elys. Blind as a bat, she said.

She looks at me, rolls her eyes, reaches for my hand, and misses it. I watch her swat the air for a second, then grab on tight. I feel like a drowning man thrown a rope. I look up at the guy to see if he's buying it. He might be, or then again, maybe not.

Before he can say anything, Elys turns around and heads through one of the cashier stands. She bangs into it as she goes.

"Ouch," she says. I try so hard not to laugh.

I hear the guy say, "That's a good one."

I'll say. I am so in love with Elys, I could kiss her like she was ketchup. Her hand tightens up as we make it back into the supermarket aisles.

"You know your glasses are too small?" I say.

"Sure, nimrod. Now, tell me what you were doing stealing. If your mom found out…" I feel panicky again.

"You aren't going to tell her?"

"I will if you don't tell me the truth right now, Terence."

How can I tell her that Lucy was stealing? I can't. Bats don't tell on bats.

"I saw someone, a friend, outside. I forgot I had the peanut butter."

"Was it that guy with the cigarettes? Did he dare you?"

"No. It wasn't him. I swear." She looks at me long and hard. Then she lets go of my hand and we walk to the shopping cart.

"Who was it, then?"

"Just this girl I know."

"Is it that girl you wanted to go to the Science

Centre with? Is she your girlfriend?"

"Get out of here."

"Is she?"

It's a good question. Is twelve too young to have a girlfriend? I mean, I haven't kissed her or anything. I haven't even thought about it. Not much, anyway. Only yesterday. Only once. Okay, maybe twice.

"She plays chess with Russell," I tell Elys.

"She must be all right then."

"Yeah, she's pretty cool."

We walk home through the park, but there's no sign of Lucy. Elys waves at Russell with a shopping bag in her hand.

"Russell said his son owns that flower shop on Vaughan and that he might be looking for someone to help out," Elys says. I never pictured Russell as a father of anybody. But then, I thought he was a pervert for a long time just because Rico said so. You never think of perverts as having families.

"Did he mean you could get a job there?"

"I think so. He's going to tell his son about me."

If Elys gets a job, who is going to take care of me? No one takes care of Lucy since Daphne got a job.

Maybe bats don't need to be taken care of. Maybe bats take care of each other.

*

Sunday morning. It's raining. I wish Tom were here so I could go hang out at his house.

I'm lying in bed worrying about Lucy and thinking about the back of her neck. Seeing a girl in her bathing suit isn't exactly the same as seeing a girl's bra, but I guess washing a girl's hair counts for something.

I wish Tom were around to talk to about it. I figure I'm about even with him now as far as girls go. He once saw this girl Frances's bra. She showed it to him when they were behind the stacks at the library.

I don't know if I should tell Tom about Lucy because then I would have to say something about her having lice which is, like, totally uncool.

9

The next morning, I shoot out of bed and up to the park. No sign of Lucy, but it's early yet. I want to tell Rico he has to find someplace else to hide those magazines. I can hardly sleep with all that ketchup under me. I don't want to be anyone's boyfriend. It's too stupid to even think of. It's like twelve-year-olds smoking. They look like monkeys — it's so ridiculous.

Why should I want to grow up so fast when all it will lead to is having to be jobless and alone all the time, or driving to Montreal with some guy with a freaky moustache?

Rico shows up.

"Hey," he says.

"Hey, what'd you do this weekend?"

"I don't know…" he says. "We went to my Nonie's up at the lake on Saturday and there was this girl there who wanted to swim with me, but my mom wouldn't let me. She said I'd get a cramp from swimming too soon after eating. She said it right in front of the girl. Unbelievable." Rico has girls on the brain.

"You have to take those magazines back," I say.

"Who needs them? I'm talking about a real, live

girl, Terence." He doesn't get what I said. "Forget it, all right? You're too young." Rico looks fed up. He goes to the Parks and Rec office to get the tetherball. He just assumes I'm going to hang out with him. Tom does that, too, except Tom's usually right.

Just then, Russell arrives in the park with his chess board under one arm and the paper under the other. I go over to the picnic table and sit down.

"Are you waiting for someone to play chess with?" I ask.

"Not if you'll play me," he says. We sit down and he starts setting up the board. I see Rico bouncing the tetherball off the side of the office up the hill. He's watching us but pretending not to. He comes down the hill and makes a big production about tying the tetherball to the pole.

I get the first move. I swear chess doesn't get interesting until at least the fourth move. Rico is being very distracting. He keeps dropping the ball and saying, "Whoops," but he's doing it on purpose.

I'm going to become a chess pro so that I don't have to deal with Rico anymore.

It gets easier to ignore him as the game goes on. Russell wins again, but I manage to get most of his best men, and I don't think he's the kind of person who lets you win, so that feels pretty good.

I go to get a drink of water from the fountain beside the wading pool. Rico comes up to me and squirts the water in my face with his thumb. He thinks he's so funny.

"That is so juvenile," I say.

"So?" he says. "What are you doing playing with the perv?"

"He's not a perv. He's got a son, you know. Just because he hangs out in the park doesn't mean he's a perv. Maybe you're the perv. You hang out in the park all the time."

"Oh, yeah? If he's not a perv, why did I see the police talking to him yesterday?"

"What?"

"They were asking him if he'd seen the Loser."

My heart falls about twenty inches into my stomach and then disappears altogether.

"What?"

"Yeah, she ran away or something. Left this big note on a piece of toilet paper. They thought maybe she was at the perv's house. They were asking all these questions." I can't believe Russell didn't say anything to me during a whole game of chess. "She's really thirteen, you know. She lied about her age because she had to stay back a year in school. She's thirteen and she still thinks she's a bat. Ha!"

"Shut up, Rico."

"What? Is she hiding out at your house? You have her hanging upside-down in your closet or something?"

"Shut up." I need time to think. Where could she be? Why didn't I come to the park yesterday? Why didn't I try to find her after going to Loblaws?

"She your girlfriend, or what?" Rico socks me one in the arm.

"Who told you?" I ask. Rico shrugs, bends over for a drink from the fountain.

"The cops were asking around about who had seen her. Don't worry. I didn't say anything about you. She's just trying to freak her parents out. Did you know she had a friend who died?"

"What?" Nobody tells me anything.

"Yeah, man. Her sister Daphne was here talking to the perv. And she was saying how Lucy had this friend in Hamilton who fell off a cliff, or maybe she jumped. I'm not sure. The kid was only nine years old. That's why Lucy's family had to leave. Lucy started acting weird all the time after her friend died. That's why she's so strange. Anyway, there's some shrink here she was seeing. Daphne felt bad because she was supposed to bring her to the shrink but didn't because she has that job at Fatso's, you know? You should have seen how hard she was bawling. The police lady had to drive her home. Like, one block."

"Did the police say anything else?" I'm thinking now about the shoplifting on Saturday. I wonder what that note said.

"Nah. They said they couldn't really do anything because she left the note. If she hadn't left a note, this place would be crawling with cops, man... that's strange about her friend, eh? From the way Daphne was talking, it's sounds like her friend was more mental than Lucy even. I wonder if she thought she could fly? Do you think that's why Lucy wears that stupid cape?"

Maybe. Maybe they were trying to fly like bats. Good thing there aren't any cliffs in this neighborhood.

"You want to play ball, or what?" Rico asks.

"Or what," I say. I run out of the park. I have an idea.

*

I'm searching through the backyard to find what I need. Two sticks. All I need are two sticks. And some paper. And some string.

Elys comes outside.

"What are you doing?"

"I'm looking," I say. I find one decent stick over by the fence.

"What are you looking for?" I bend the stick to test its give, and it breaks. I throw the pieces back on the ground.

I should have told Elys about Lucy's house last week. I should have said something at Loblaws. I thought I was being a good bat. It's my fault. Now I have to get her back.

"Terence? Can I help you look?" I look up at Elys. I don't know what to tell her, so I keep looking. I poke the ground with my shoes. "I got an interview at the flower shop."

"What?" I say. I stop looking.

"I talked to that guy. Russell's son. You know, the florist? He seems really nice. Very casual. He wants me to go up there this afternoon to talk about a job. He says Russell told him all about me. So I say to the guy, 'I only met him for ten minutes,' and he says, 'Well, he liked you and my dad is a hard guy to impress. And this is wedding season, and I need someone.' I think I have a real chance this time. A flower shop, too. Isn't that great?" She looks so happy.

There's no way I can tell her about Lucy now. I don't want her to be all freaked out for the first job interview she's had in weeks.

"Now, what can I help you with?"

"I need a kite," I tell her. She looks at me kind of strangely.

"I think there's an old one of mine down in the basement." We go down there and Elys pulls out this old handmade kite with sparkles all over it. "I made it in grade four. Don't you remember me bringing it over a couple of years ago? You said it was pathetic."

"Did I? Well, I was wrong, Elys. It's perfect." It's made out of plain brown paper. "Do we have any markers?"

"You're going to ruin my kite?"

"I'm going to improve it. I swear. I'll never say anything you do is pathetic ever again if you give me this kite."

"Is this the new craze up at the park?"

"Something like that."

*

"You're going to fly a kite?" Rico asks as I'm crossing through the park. "You sure have turned strange the last couple of weeks. First I find you playing chess with the perv…"

I have a plan, but I don't want to say anything to Rico. Not with the way his brain works. I can't do anything without that guy laughing at me. I wish Tom were here, to put him in his place. Then again, I don't. Probably if Tom were here he and Rico would go off to smoke and read dirty magazines, which is what I should be doing anyway. But I'm not cool. I like bats, and I like chess, and I like Lucy. I'm not cool and that's just too bad for the rest of the world.

Rico starts to follow me across the park. I stop. The last thing I need is for him to come along.

"I swear, all I want to do is fly the damn kite," I tell him.

I run away from him with the stupid sparkly paper kite trailing behind me. By the lights near Loblaws I look back and see him watching me. I slow down crossing the street and try to look casual.

Before the light changes, I see a police car coming around the other side of the park.

Man, I got out of there just in time. I don't know how to talk to the police, and, after the peanut-butter incident the other day, I'm in no mood for an on-the-spot lesson.

By the time I get to the ravine it's pretty cloudy. It isn't a good day to be flying a kite. I've got to contact Lucy, though. I hope she didn't run away because I got caught at Loblaws.

In the middle of the field, I take the marker out. It doesn't work as well as I'd hoped. I have to keep licking the end to get the marker stuff out of it. I draw an outline of a bat on the kite. I have to be careful not to poke through the paper.

The kite is going to be the bat signal. If she sees it, she'll know it's me. Who else flies a dorky paper kite in the middle of a rainstorm? It hasn't started to rain yet, but I can tell it's going to soon.

I can't tell which way the wind is going. It seems to be all over the place. I can't get the thing to fly at all. I run around the hill, just like Rico did the other day. If Lucy were here, we'd be able to get this thing up in the air. But if Lucy were here, I wouldn't need to.

It's raining now. Not very hard. But it's raining. I could get electrocuted through this kite. Lucy would see it for sure if it got struck by lightning and burst into flames in the sky.

I have to stop and catch my breath. I flop down on my back and watch the storm clouds gather over my head. It rains on my face so that I can't tell what's sweat and what's not. It's more like mist than rain. It's like when Steel, Tom's dog, breathes on you. Steel won't let me near Tom when I go over there to play. What kind of dog guards a kid from his best friend? I used to think I wanted a dog, but then I met Steel. He also farts a lot and nobody says anything about it. Tom's whole living room can be full of dog farts and everyone still pretends the air tastes like ice cream. It's how I know every house has its own gaps. Some houses have bigger gaps than others.

You could fly a blimp through the gaps in Lucy's house.

I hold the kite above my face to keep from getting so wet. I feel the wind lift it from my hands. I scramble to my feet. The wind is all over the place but the bat is hanging on, going up in jigs and jags. It's still raining. The clouds are low and heavy. They look like the bottoms of ships floating slowly through the sky. If I were a kite I would ride one.

I'm all over the hill again trying to keep up with the thing. I can't take my eyes off it. The rain is running down my face. The drops fall right in my eyes. I blink a few times to get them out, and when I look back up again, the kite has disappeared into the clouds. I wind the line up a bit. I can feel it stretching. It's too sharp to hang onto without gloves. I run around the hill trying to see the kite. I hear thunder. I could seriously get electrocuted. I should get the kite down and try again later, only I can't even see it anymore. I feel the wind pick up.

The rain starts to fall like thousands of hard pins, so that I feel like I'm being grated like cheese. I take my shirt off and wrap it around my hands. The rain stabs me all over. I pull hard on the line, putting one hand over the other and jerking it down. A huge peal of thunder rolls across the sky and through me. I almost let go right then. I want to put my hands over my head to keep the sky from falling on me, but I've got to get the kite down.

Finally, it comes back into view. It must be soaking. It's amazing it's still up there. I give three more huge pulls and the thing starts into a nose dive. I drop the line and the whole sky lights up like Christmas. I fall flat on my stomach and hug the ground for all I'm worth.

10

I'm face down forever before the rain calms down. I can't see my shirt. It must have drowned. There are puddles all over the ravine.

Everyone at Wells Hill Park is probably hanging out under the tree. I bet Russell didn't even stop playing chess. I can't believe he didn't say anything to me about Lucy. He must live in chess world. No wonder he looks all put out when I take his big guys off the board. I could be some sort of young chess genius. I could be a prodigy.

It's hard knowing you are a completely ordinary guy. When Tom's around, I feel like somebody because I know I'm Tom's friend. He always seems to know what to do. When I'm with Tom, it's easy to fill the gaps in the day because I just do whatever Tom does. Even that day with Rico, at least I didn't have to think about what to do with myself.

I never used to think I had any interests apart from gin rummy and tetherball. Now I know I like chess, bats and kites. Actually, I think liking bats is a separate thing from being one.

I go out to the field to find my shirt. My shoes are soaked and squishing with bubbles with every step.

I can feel kind of a slime build-up between my toes. Totally gross.

I don't find my shirt until I have already stepped on it. It looks like one of those shirts you sometimes see run over on the highway.

I can't put the shirt on, so I tie it around my waist. My hair is all wet, too, so I slick it back off my face. It feels good.

I find the end of the kite line and start pulling it in. I reel it in about ten feet and then it snags. I can't see the kite. I have no idea where it landed.

I follow the line to the edge of a hill. I look down into the ravine, but there's no sign of the kite. There's a steep hill down to the next level of the ravine. It's almost a cliff. I mean, I'm walking down sideways and the drop is like a wall beside me. I have to grab hold of the grass a few times to keep myself from slipping in the muck.

I follow the kite line to just under the bridge where Spadina Road goes over the ravine. I remember Lucy saying how bats lived under bridges. I can't see any up in the iron work there. I don't know where they would roost.

I wind the line up some more, wondering where it will lead me.

"Is this what you're looking for, batbrain?" And, like magic, there's Lucy holding the kite at the side of the bridge.

"I knew bats lived here," I say. Thank God she's all right! I don't know what to say next. I stand there half-naked, with this big goofy smile on my face.

Lucy has a green scarf tied around her head. She isn't one bit wet. I try to cover my chest with my arms.

"Is anyone with you?" she says.

"No. I was just flying a kite. You know…" It's no use trying to cover my chest. My arms are too skinny. It would be too obvious to put my shirt back on, too. I guess I'll just have to be naked.

"Did you get in trouble the other day?" she asks. She walks down toward me from the side of the bridge and hands me the kite. It's all wrecked, but you can still see the bat on it. I use it to cover my chest like some kind of shield.

"No. My cousin was there. She made like I was looking for her." Lucy smiles. She doesn't smile that often. It's like someone turned a light on in her head.

We hear another a peal of thunder. It echoes under the bridge.

"Come on," she says. I follow Lucy up the side of the bridge. She pushes aside a bush and I can see an arch under this part of the bridge. She crawls into it and looks back to make sure I'm with her.

It's dark in here, and it takes my eyes a while to adjust. I feel the wall with my hand. It's jagged where the bridge has worn away.

I hear Lucy light a match, and the whole cave lights up. I can see the iron work of the bridge above us. No bats, though. Well, none except Lucy.

The whole space is no bigger than my bathroom, with way less head room. I can't stand up. There's a sleeping bag in the corner with a bunch of blankets underneath it and a bunch of newspapers underneath that. Three boxes of emergency candles sit by the bed. The lit one sits in a crevice just above a full knapsack. At the foot of the bed is a huge pot with a lid on it and beside that is a plastic Loblaws bag full of chip wrappers and Coke cans. In the middle of the floor are two books: the one Lucy showed me about bats, and the one on kites that she got the Moran/midget story out of.

"Welcome to my home." Lucy plops herself down on the bed. She's not wearing her bat sheet anymore. The candle makes long shadows of her legs on the wall.

"I'm surprised you found me," she says. "But not really surprised. Bats have a great sense of smell. In a cave of a thousand bats, we can always find our friends. You probably found me because we click." She starts clicking her tongue at me like it's supposed to mean something to me.

"I was looking for you, actually." Lucy is jiggling her leg against the floor in that way that it would shake the whole floor if it were actually a floor and not dirt. That green bandanna is really kooky. It could be some kind of bat thing. Maybe it's to keep the lice off her shoulders. "Everyone is looking for you, Lucy."

"Did you hear me? Every bat has its own click. So even in an area of thousands of bats we still know —"

"The police are looking for you..."

"You must have heard my clicks, because otherwise you wouldn't be here, right? I saw the kite and I knew it was you. I mean, only bats know how to find each other with clicking. Only bats know how to hang tough together." She is talking a mile a minute. She doesn't seem to hear what I told her about the police.

"Rico told me about your note. What did it say?" She looks at me like I'm speaking another language and starts clicking her tongue again. "You didn't say anything about Loblaws, did you? That's not why you left?" She shakes her head and brings her face right up into mine, clicking. I don't know what to do, so I pick up the bat book and start flipping through it.

She sits down beside me and pulls it away.

"I'm hiding from the enemy. I don't want to get my eyes poked out. I don't want to be locked in the dark with a bunch of owls." Now she's talking crazy talk. She has these vibes coming off her like she's had too much coffee, all shivery and tense. I want to put my arm around her, but I don't want her to think that I want her to be my girlfriend, even though she might be already. It seems like a better idea to let her be a bat for a while. She'll get tired of it.

Lucy takes the book from me.

"It says here that this Italian scientist, Lazzaro Spallanzani, sealed all these bats and owls together in a dark room to see how they would fly in the dark. The owls bashed into everything, but the bats could find their way around no problem. So then Spallanzani blindfolds the bats to see if they can still get around, and, of course they do, because we use echoes to find out where everything is. Like we yell like this: OOOOOOOOOO." She hollers so loud, I'm sure the cars on the bridge can hear. Somebody's gonna find us if she goes on like that. I want to put my hand over her mouth, but she lifts up her finger and stops. "Did you hear that?"

"How could I not hear that?"

"I mean the echo, Terence." She looks at me for a second and then dives back into the book. "Spallanzani didn't know about echoes and how we can tell how close something is just by yelling at it and hearing the sound bounce off it. You shouldn't put blindfolds on animals. I don't think you should try to make anything blind that isn't already. Anyway, it didn't work, did it? But Spallanzani couldn't leave it at that. He goes and pokes our bat eyes out and then sends us out into the night to see if we can find our way home. And we did find our way home and he still wasn't happy. He murdered a bunch of us bats — ones with eyes, ones without eyes, didn't matter to him. He murdered us and cut open our stomachs to see if the bats with eyes ate the same amount as the bats without eyes. And you know what he found?"

I have a picture in my head of gutted, blinded bats and this guy, Spallanzani, leaning over them with blood on his hands.

"What?"

"Nothing. The bats with eyes and the bats without eyes ate the same amount. He killed them for nothing. How could he do that? How could he poke their eyes out and cut their stomachs open? He shouldn't have done that."

I see a drop fall on the book. At first I look up at the ceiling to see if there is a leak. Then I realize it's Lucy crying. I put my arm around her shoulder.

"What a Moran," I say. She looks at me and gives a half-smile.

"He's worse than a Moran. He's a Spallanzani. Those owls in that dark room, they bumped into everything and he didn't do anything to them. It's not fair to be picked on because you're smart like a bat." Lucy tugs on the end of the bandanna on her head and wipes her eye with a corner of it. I take my shirt from around my waist and give it to her to cry into. I can still hear the rain rustling the bush outside.

"You want some spaghetti?" she asks.

"I didn't know bats ate spaghetti."

"This bat does." Lucy moves over to where the pot is. She puts it between us and lifts up the lid. There's a whole pot full of spaghetti in there. She digs a fork out of her knapsack and hands it to me. I shouldn't really eat her food.

"Why did you run away?" I know it's a dangerous question. She might start clicking again.

"I didn't run away. I migrated. Bats migrate when it gets too cold where they are. That apartment was freezing. We can't fly unless we're at the right temperature."

It's almost August. The whole city's stinking hot. Last year, Tom and me tried to fry an egg on the sidewalk — and it almost worked.

"Is that what you said in the note? That you were migrating?"

"What are you so obsessed with that note for? It wasn't about you. Everybody always thinks everything is about them. All I said was that I had to go away for a while until things warmed up. I couldn't stand listening to everything freezing up like that."

"What do you mean?"

"I mean, we did all that work cleaning the apartment and nobody said anything. It's like the whole place doesn't even exist."

I think I know what she means. It's like when I asked Mom about going to canoe camp with Tom and she said maybe, and then never mentioned it again. And now it's summer and Tom is gone and I'm still here — all without anybody saying anything.

At least I have Elys to take care of me. Nobody takes care of Lucy. Except maybe me.

She's not going to be able to live long on this spaghetti.

"You should come to my house," I say. I take a forkful of spaghetti. I'm starving. If she comes home with me, I'll make her some wieners and macaroni. "We've got an extra bedroom. I'm sure it'd be okay with my mom."

Her eyes fill with tears again. I wonder if bats cry. This one does. Too much.

"I can't. I can't."

"Why not?"

Lucy crosses over to the bed. She turns her back to me and unwraps the bandanna from around her head.

My heart does something it's never done before. It flops over four full times, like a fish fresh out of water.

Lucy is bald. She's shaved her head. And I can tell

she had a hard time doing it because there are a few nicks by her ear and at the base of her neck. She must have done it to get rid of the lice.

Oh, Lucy. I can see her neck muscles tighten. I swear, I can see her brain thinking. She lets her face fall in her hands.

I can't catch my breath. I remember the color of her hair. How I once thought it was spiky and stringy, and also how it burned like fire. And also, how I touched it.

"Lucy." I don't know what to say. "Lucy. It'll grow back, Lucy."

She shakes her head in her hands. She can't face me. I don't blame her. I go over to her and slowly, slowly, put my hand on her head. I feel her relax under me. She lets out a sob that sounds like the tip of a tidal wave of tears. She buries her face in the sleeping bag and sobs like the end of the world is coming. I sit beside her and pat her back.

I say, "Shh, shh."

We sit like that for a long time. I listen to the rain outside. I listen to myself say "shh." The candle burns down a bit. I think about how stupid it is to worry about having a weenie chest or getting caught smoking. I think about how those ketchup magazines under my mattress are so fake. I think about Tom's dog Steel and how he farts up a storm and the whole house stinks and how they love that dog any-

113

way. And I think about how it must feel to be so lonely like Lucy and how, I guess, sometimes I feel that way.

I almost feel like crying, too. Only, I also have the feeling that the rain is crying for me and Lucy both. I feel like the whole day is a crying day.

The candle goes out. I have no idea what time it is. Lucy is asleep. I should let her sleep. I sit there in the dark until my eyes adjust to the light.

I can make out the edges of Lucy's face. Her head looks so small without hair. *She* looks so much smaller when she's asleep. She almost looks like a normal girl, except without hair.

Tom might not think that Lucy is pretty. Her nose is too long and pointy, and her eyes are set deep in her head so that her cheeks seem to bloom out of them. Her eyebrows are slightly knotted together, as if she were trying to balance something on top of her head. Her bald head.

I see the marker lying on the ground by the books. I crawl over and get it. I rip a piece off the kite and write Lucy a note.

"Dear Lucy Bat, I will be back later with food. Please stay here." I was going to sign it "Terence Bat," but the marker finally gave out.

I crawl out into the ravine and scramble up the other side of the bridge. I don't want to go back through the park. I don't want to have to talk to the

114

police if they are still there. Rico will probably tell them I don't know anything anyway.

All the way home I think about what I could make to take to Lucy. I'll have to give Elys some lame excuse for going out again. She'll let me, though. She trusts me not to get into trouble. I think I'll make Lucy a bunch of cheese sandwiches with those simulated cheese flats. Those things'll last forever — however long that is.

*

When I get home, Mom is sitting on the sofa with her feet up on the coffee table.

"Where have you been?" she asks. Her voice is calm but I get the feeling like something has happened.

"I was at the park," I say. She takes her feet off the coffee table and leans forward on her elbows. Something has definitely happened.

"Just tell me where you were, Terence. I know you weren't at the park." I wonder if she went looking for me. That's odd. I think of something else.

"What time is it?"

"Answer the question." I go and sit in the rocking chair.

"Where's Elys?"

"Terence!" She's standing up now. I haven't seen her this angry in a long time. She must have found the magazines. Or maybe Elys told her about the smoking. "I'll ask you again. Where were you?"

"I was in the park. I swear it."

"No, you weren't. Try again."

"Not Wells Hill Park, Mom. The other one. The ravine. Up by Spadina. I was flying a kite."

She seems to deflate a little.

"In the rain? That's dangerous."

"I know, but..."

"God, I was so worried. The police were here, you know. They were looking for some girl. What's her name?"

"Lucy."

"That's right. Do you know her?"

"Kind of...you're home early today."

"It's past eight, Terence. I've been home for two hours already. I don't want you out this late alone, all right? We don't know what happened to that girl."

She doesn't know what happened to that girl.

"I want you home at five o'clock every day. I know it's a bummer, but I can't have you tooling about the neighborhood on your own if there's some freak out there. I'm going to be coming home a lot earlier and I want you to be here."

"That's not fair." I say it to myself, but Mom hears me.

"What's that?" I can feel my face getting red. Somebody needs me, and now Mom's pulling this stupid adult trip on me. A five o'clock curfew and I didn't even do anything.

"There's no freak out there, Mom. She ran away... I mean, Rico told me she ran away." I have to be careful not to spill the beans. I'm rocking the chair really fast now. "Elys would let me stay out." I think I hurt her feeling with that one. She sits back down again.

"Well, I'm not Elys, am I?" she says finally. "Elys has a new job and she isn't going to be around so much anymore. That's why I'm coming home earlier."

Everything's changing so fast. Who am I going to watch television with? Mom? I'm going to eat stupid hot dogs for the rest of my life because that's all Mom can cook.

"I guess that won't leave you much time for Farley." It was a stupid thing to say. I want to piss her off. I want her to feel bad like me.

She doesn't even say anything. She just stands up and walks to the kitchen.

"There's some lasagna for you in the oven."

Elys must have made it for me. My favorite food and I don't even feel like eating.

I stop the rocking chair and head for the kitchen. What a rotten day this turned out to be. "And wipe that black gunk off your tongue. What have you been doing, eating charcoal?"

11

When I wake up the next morning, the house is empty. For once, it doesn't seem like all that many hours between nine and five. I root around the house for things to take Lucy. I should show my face up at Wells Hill Park today. Try to find out what's going on at Lucy's house.

I get a big knapsack from the basement and start filling it with stuff: a pillow, a blanket, a flashlight, a big jar of cranberry juice, my Swiss army knife, a toothbrush and some toothpaste squeezed into a baggie, a pack of playing cards, a crummy harmonica I got in my Christmas stocking last year and a whole shopping bag full of cheese sandwiches (some with mayonnaise and some without).

I get halfway down the block with the whole heavy pack and turn back for some fruit and celery. Lucy should try to eat a balanced diet to keep up her strength.

I take the back way into the ravine so that I won't have to go through the park. That way I can just cruise into Wells Hill later with no load on my back and make like I just slept in.

My knapsack jams in the mouth of the cave and I fall flat on my face.

"Oof." I crawl the rest of the way inside. I can't see anything.

"Lucy?"

No answer. I open the knapsack and fish out the flashlight. I turn it on and beam it on the bed. It's lumpy. I go over and nudge the lump, but it's just the sleeping bag. Empty.

Oh, no. She moved! Where could she have gone? Maybe there is some freak wandering around. I shouldn't have let her stay here. I should have taken her home, bald head or no bald head.

I beam the flashlight around, looking for clues. I look in the pot of spaghetti and see that it's all gone. She must have been hungry. Maybe she went out to steal some food. I hope not. What if she gets caught? What are they going to make of a little bald bat stealing chips?

It looks like she's still here. The strand of spaghetti on the bottom of the pot is still kind of wet, so she couldn't have eaten it that long ago.

I leave the knapsack and crawl out of the cave. Halfway out I feel a hard blow on the back of my neck and fall flat on my face again.

"Terence! I'm so sorry." I look up at her, but I can hardly see through the flapping wings of the little birdies flying around my head. "I saw lights in the cave and thought maybe the police were in there. I was going to hide, but you came out too quick. Are you okay?"

119

"Okay?" I try to get to my feet and knock my head on the top of the cave entrance. "Owwww." Lucy pushes me back inside and onto the bed. I hear some fumbling about and then the light goes on.

"What did you bring me?" She's over by the knapsack and unloading it in a hurry. She has the bandanna back on her head. She looks like a gypsy fairy in the half-light of the cave.

"Pass me the pillow," I say. My head smarts something fierce.

"Celery?" She says it like it's a dirty word.

"Cheese sandwiches, too. You have to keep your strength up."

"Yeah, yeah. Bats eat insects. That's all bats need. But thanks. Your mom buys good bread. We always get the white stuff. I mean, that's what they have in their apartment."

My head hurts badly. What if it were the police in here? She would have knocked the police on the head.

"You should go home, Lucy. It's not safe here. I'm sure your family won't care about your hair."

She keeps unloading the knapsack like she hasn't heard me. She pulls out the Swiss army knife.

"Excellent. This is exactly what I need."

Now I'm sorry I brought all this stuff. Especially the knife. What if she stabs someone trying to come into the cave? I'll be an accessory to murder.

"When are you going to go home?"

She gives the harmonica a try. It sounds awful.

"You know, baby bats that can't hold onto their mothers fall to the bottom of the cave and are eaten by predators who are just waiting there for them to fall down. It's no wonder they hold on so tight. You have to learn how to fly on your own really early. That way if you fall it's no big deal because you can fly, right?"

I'm not following her. She's talking like a bat again. Maybe I should tell someone she's here. I don't want her to hate me, but she might be in trouble. In the head, I mean.

"Are you going to go home?" I say.

Finally, she turns away from the knapsack to face me. She flips through the attachments on the Swiss army knife: a knife, a saw, a magnifying glass, a can opener, a corkscrew and some short, sharp pointy thing. She flicks them back in and looks at me.

"Thanks for bringing the stuff. I have a plan, you know. I have a really important project I'm working on. I have a lot of work to do. A lot of work…do you have a tape measure? Because that would really help." She looks around at all the stuff. "A tape measure and a big sheet of heavy plastic — like a drop sheet for paint. I need a lot of stuff, actually. I think I got good branches this morning." She tugs at something at the door and brings it into the light. She has two huge branches.

121

"What are you making?"

"You gave me the idea with the kite yesterday. I've got to do something. I can't just sit back and let us all die. It will throw off the whole ecosystem. Did you know bats eat fifty percent of their body weight in bugs every day? Well, the ones who eat bugs. The ones who eat fruit help pollinate the fruit trees, just like bees. And they're killing us, Terence. They think we have rabies. They're scared of us. They aren't thinking. They don't know what we do for the world." She has this stunned look on her face. Her head is practically drowning in the bandanna.

"You're making a kite? For...why are you making a kite?" I sit up straight.

"It's like that Moran guy, only it's going to be me flying. It's time for me to fly, Terence. And I'm not going to be screaming for people to buy candy bars. I'm going to be saving bats."

"I don't get it."

"I'm going to make a huge kite and paint it with the message Save the Bats, and I'm going to fly it all over town and everywhere where bats are endangered."

I am stunned.

"You can't do that. I mean, I've heard of Save the Whales and Save the Seals and Save the Rain Forest, but Save the Bats? Forget it. It's like Save the Mosquito. People just won't go for it. Plus there's no way you're going to build a kite that will carry you. No way."

It all just bursts out of me. Someone has got to bring her back to earth.

"You don't believe in anything, do you, Terence?" She says this like she feels sorry for me.

"I do, too."

"Like what? What do you believe in?"

I think hard. What do I believe? I never really thought about it before. I believe that there are gaps in the world that someone should get around to filling in. I believe it's not cool to pretend to be anything you aren't, except…don't I like Lucy and isn't Lucy pretending she's a bat? The way she's looking at me with those laser eyes of hers, it seems important that I believe in something.

"I believe in believing," is what I end up saying. It is all I can think of that is true, and if there's one person in the world I couldn't ever say one false thing to, it's Lucy.

"Good," she says. "I believe in bats, and I believe in kites. If you believe in believing, then you should believe in me." And with that she opens up the Swiss army knife and starts whittling at one of the branches. "Bats are a really important part of the ecosystem, Terence. Seals? Seals are practically useless. They eat all the fish and don't do anything. Just because they're all cute and white when they're little — that's the only reason people want to save them. You shouldn't be picked on just because you're ugly. People just don't understand bats. They kill them because they aren't beautiful like cats or seals." She whittles away.

Why shouldn't I believe in Lucy? Why not bats? My whole summer's been turned upside-down since I became a bat. I don't know about anything anymore.

I watch Lucy whittle the branch. She's good with the knife. She has this concentrated look on her face, like nothing's going to stop her, and I guess that includes me.

"I think bats are beautiful," I say.

Lucy keeps on whittling like she didn't hear me say anything.

I should go to Wells Hill Park and show my face, see if anyone can tell me what the police have been up to.

"I gotta go soon. What did you say you needed again?" She doesn't even look up.

"Tape measure, a big piece of plastic sheeting, string, glue, tape —"

"Hold on, hold on. How about I come back later with a pen and paper and we figure it out?"

"Fine," she looks up again. It'll be hard working in the dark. "Thanks a lot, Terence. You're good." I slip out of the cave — careful not to hit my head this time — and make my way toward the park.

She said I'm good. It must be true. Lucy never says anything that isn't true. She may be a thief, but she's not a liar.

12

I get to the park and, for the first time ever, Russell isn't there. The picnic table looks naked without him.

I go to get a drink at the water fountain and see Rico and Daphne sitting on a bench down the hill. Daphne has long dark-brown hair that falls down her back like a horse's tail. She's not exactly pretty, except in that way that older girls seem to be prettier. They look better-cooked or something, like those pictures of steaks you see with the grill marks on them.

I look at the birthmark on the side of Daphne's face. It looks like someone threw grape juice at her. I wonder what she thinks of Lucy putting tattoos on her face on purpose when she's never going to be able to get rid of that thing. It looks like she has a permanent black eye. She wears all these bracelets on both her arms that make her look like a prisoner. She always hunches her shoulders forward, too, as if she had a knapsack on even though she doesn't.

I go down the hill toward them. Rico looks at me and juts out his chin. I try to look like I don't know anything.

"Hey, Terence, seen Lucy?"

I shrug. I'm not a good liar.

"She hasn't come home yet?" I ask. Daphne shakes her head.

"My parents are freaking out. It's worse than last time. Way, way worse. I can't even work now because my hands are shaking so bad I keep flipping the Fatso burgers on the ground."

"Have the police found anything?"

"No…and they say they can't do anything because she's a runaway. It would be different if she didn't leave the note. I should have never said anything about the note. Rico said the two of you were good friends. Did she say anything to you about going any place?"

I want to spill my guts, but I promised Lucy. Or did I? It feels like I did.

"She didn't say she was going anywhere. I saw her at Loblaws on Friday." Daphne gets this hopeful look on her face. She would be perfectly pretty if it weren't for that birthmark. Only the birthmark makes me want to look at her longer.

"What time was that?"

"I don't know. Three-thirty maybe. Something like that." She looks over at Loblaws as if looking there is going to make Lucy come out.

I want to tell her so bad. I can't. I'm here to gather information.

"Did you tell the cops that?" Rico asks. He seems

way more concerned than he was yesterday. "I sent the cops to your house."

"Yeah. My mom talked to them. I wasn't there. Thanks a lot, Rico. Now my mom thinks there's some psychotic killer on the loose and I have to be home by five."

"Oh, my God," says Daphne. She puts a hand over her mouth. I can see tears forming in her eyes.

What a stupid thing to say. I always say the wrong thing.

"I know she's all right," I say. "I mean, I have a feeling she's fine. I mean, Lucy's really smart. She knows how to play chess and everything. She can take care of herself." And she can steal, and she can find caves, and she's got my knife which I hope she doesn't use to take out any snooping cops while I'm gone.

My words aren't working to calm Daphne down. Her face is all pale and tense.

"I should have come home when she called. Oh, my God. I can't believe we left her alone so long. She called me and I didn't come. She must have been so angry. And all I could think about was that my stunned boss would be mad about me taking a personal call. If I knew she...I just know I could have stopped her going. We should know better by now."

"That wasn't why she left," I say.

Daphne whips her head up. Rico stands up and creeps closer to me.

"What?" he says. It's like he's suddenly Daphne's boyfriend or something. But she's seventeen so there's no way. Still, he's so big. I have to think fast.

"I mean, she didn't say anything to me about calling you," I tell Daphne. "I think she would have said something to me."

"Are you her boyfriend?" Daphne asks. I want to say yes and I want to say no. Rico's looking at me like my answer could change his life.

"I'm a bat. Like Lucy. We're bats together. That's all." Rico rolls his eyes and sits back down. Daphne's face lights up through her tears. She grabs my hand and squeezes it. I said something right for once. And I *do* feel like a bat. I'm flying through these gaps like I know exactly where to go. I feel myself relax a little inside. On the inside it feels kind of like I'm being unfolded.

"Did she run away before?" I ask. Daphne shakes her head.

"Not exactly. It's a really long story." It must be the one Rico was telling me — about Lucy's friend who fell off the cliff.

"What happened? I mean, I might be able to remember something if you told me what happened."

Daphne falls back against the bench.

"When we lived in Hamilton, there was this girl who lived near us who was a really good friend of Lucy's. Her name was Timber. Actually, her name was Tammy, but she liked to be called Timber. And one day, we were out on the Escarpment and we were just playing, right? Then Timber went off the edge and there was nothing we could do and she died." Daphne stops to take a couple of deep breaths. "It happened so fast. I don't know. I think Timber thought she *was* a tree. Her father was this conservationist. You know, a save-the-trees guy."

Daphne is talking almost like she is in some trance. She's staring at Loblaws the whole time.

"We were looking for robins' eggs. She was there when I looked down, and when I looked up she was gone. I just knew right away that she had gone over the edge. She fell like timber." Daphne chokes a bit. "I don't think it was deliberate. Not exactly. At least, I don't think it was planned…it was a long drop. She hit her head on a rock. I sent Lucy to call 911, but I knew she was dead.

"That's when Lucy started being a bat. She was never a bat before Timber died. And Mom and Dad were working hard then. Working all the time, just like now."

She stops to take a breath. Rico hands her a napkin. Looks like he picked it up at the 7-11.

"We couldn't find Lucy for dinner one time. It was really weird. We were hardly ever all together for dinner and Mom had made this whole big deal about how we were all going to be together for dinner and everything. And it wasn't even until we were sitting around the table that we realize she's not there. We just thought she'd show up because it was this whole big deal. So, of course, Mom freaks out and then Dad yells at Mom for freaking out and I go out looking for her. I go up the Escarpment looking for her..." Daphne starts sobbing again.

What would I do if Tom died? I don't know how to be that sad.

"Mom calls Timber's father to see if she's over there. And we're all thinking she's gone off the edge, just like Timber."

Daphne looks down at her hands and wipes her eyes with the 7-11 napkin. "And then, Mom is in Lucy's room looking around, and she hears something up in the attic." This is the part I know already. "There's this hole in Lucy's closet up to the attic. Mom goes up there and it's dark and all she can see is something swinging. She nearly has a heart attack. Dad gets home and hears Mom screaming upstairs. He races up and she points up into the attic, so he has a look and when I come in he's running down the stairs with this look on his face...I'll never forget it as long as I live. And I start screaming just from looking at him. He gets the flashlight and goes back up to the attic and there she is. Lucy's hanging from the rafters, but she's hanging from her feet. And you know what she says to my dad?"

"What?" me and Rico say at once.

"She says, 'Turn off the light.'"

Neither me or Rico can speak. Daphne's looking far off into outer space. It seems more quiet than it can be with the traffic rushing by the park like this.

Then I want to tell her everything. I want to tell her that Lucy is fine and that she'll be home soon. Only I don't know that for sure.

13

When I get home, Elys is there.

"What are you doing here?" I ask her. "I thought you had a job."

"I don't know. What are you doing here?" She's on the couch with her feet up on the coffee table reading some flyers. She likes to keep up on the good deals even though she never buys anything.

"I live here, remember?"

"Oh, yeah. Aunt Paulie said I might see some short stringy kid with hair in his face and an attitude problem wandering around. You must be him." I flop down beside her on the couch.

"I thought you got a job. Mom's making me come home by five. It's like in her head I'm still eight years old." I grab a Zellers flyer and try to find the toy section.

"Oooh. Bummer, man. I am, like, soooo sorry that I got a great job that pays decent money *and* is just up the street *and* the boss lets me go home for lunch or between making deliveries *and* there's a tape deck in the delivery van *and* it's all thanks to your friend Russell."

"Did your new boss tell you about Lucy?"

"What about her?" she says.

"She ran away."

She quits poking me.

"What?"

"Yeah. She ran away after we saw her at Loblaws and they can't find her. The cops were here and they were talking to Russell, too."

"What were they talking to him for?"

"I don't know. She plays chess with him sometimes."

"Do they think he took her or something?"

"I don't know. That's why I was wondering if your boss said anything to you. Because Russell wasn't at the park today."

Elys looks at her watch. I haven't seen her look at her watch in months. I forgot she even had a watch.

"I gotta get back. Lunch is almost over. David's pretty cool, but he's still a boss and it is my first day on the job." She gets up and checks her hair in the mirror. She's wearing it back today. It makes her look more like a grown-up. "What did you say your friend's name was?"

"Lucy." She looks at her watch again, and then makes for the door.

"I'll ask my boss about your friend. I hope Russell isn't in any kind of trouble."

I have myself a hot dog and cheese sandwich and make out a list of the things Lucy wants me to get her: a tape measure, plastic...

I did see some plastic somewhere. It was in that lady's garage, the one where Rico hid the magazines. It was stuck in the rafters there.

It's not like she's using it. It's only plastic. I could take the magazines back there and get the plastic at the same time.

I look up at the clock. It's gone 2:30 already. I'd better get a move on. I get the magazines and stuff them, bag and all, down the back of my pants, just like I saw Lucy do with the spaghetti. I wouldn't want to fall down and have them all spill out of the bag. Man, oh, man. What a nightmare.

I run up Bathurst and cut through to the alley behind Rico's street. At first I'm not sure if I'm in the right alley. They all look the same, with the garages backing off bushy backyards with laundry lines, and totally deserted except for cats.

I like alleys. They're like secret streets, like visible gaps. No one ever talks about them, but there they are just the same — places between places.

Now that I'm here, it doesn't seem like such a good idea to go into the lady's garage. It was one thing when I was following Rico. I felt like if we got caught it would be Rico's fault, or maybe I felt like we wouldn't get caught because Rico was with me.

I look up and down the alley. Then I pull on the bottom of the door. It's locked, all right. I get on my knees and peek under the crack under the door.

It's empty, so at least I know she's not home. But it's not as dark as it should be. I see a crack of light coming from the far end. It's hard to see, but I think the door to the backyard is open. I can get in through the lady's backyard.

Just as I'm walking down the lane between the two houses, I hear, "What the hell do you think you're doing, batboy?" I grab the back of my pants and turn around to face Rico.

"Hey, Rico." I try to act casual.

"What are you doing here? Are you looking for me?"

"Any news about Lucy?" I say. He shakes his head and looks at my arm resting behind my back. I whip it back at my side.

"What have you got there?"

"Nothing."

"That's bull, bathead. Pass it over. Come on...I know you're hiding something and I'm gonna get it out of you one way or another."

I pull out the bag and hand it over. I feel so much lighter once he has the magazines in his hands.

"What am I supposed to do with these?" he says.

"That's your problem." It is his problem and it feels good to say it. He looks at me and looks down at the bag and looks up at his house.

"Why'd you bring these back here?"

"I didn't want them around. You saw my cousin.

She knows I have them. I don't want her thinking I'm looking at them all the time. Every time she looks at me now, it's like all she sees is me reading dirty magazines."

I spit this all out really fast. I didn't even know that's what I was thinking until I spit it out like that.

He puts his hand to his mouth to show me to be quiet.

"Well...what were you going to do with them?"

"I was going to put them back in that lady's garage. The front door is open."

Rico raises his eyebrows. It's like he hadn't even thought of the front door before. I mean, duh.

"All right, then, batbrain. Go ahead." He tries to hand me the bag. I put my hands behind my back and clench my fists.

"No way, Rico. You got me into this mess. You put them back."

Rico lets out a deep breath, walks to the end of his house and looks into his neighbor's yard. He walks back.

"I'll only come on one condition," I say.

"What?"

"You help me get some plastic from up in the rafters."

"What?" He looks at me like I'm speaking Martian.

"Listen, you get me in trouble and then you run

off and leave me holding the bag. I went down for you, man. You owe me." They talk this way on television. On television, it's the good guy who is owed the favor and he always gets it. It's the television rule, but I don't know if it's the life rule.

My heart's bubbling like hot spaghetti sauce. I need the plastic for Lucy. I guess I don't technically owe her anything, but I feel like I do.

"Fine," he says. The rule works.

I follow him down to the end of the houses and watch him make sure the coast is clear. Now I really feel like I'm on television.

We go through his neighbor's gate and race to the garage door and inside. We stop and hold our breaths to see if there's any fallout. Nothing. Rico hides the magazines back in the pipe. I feel way better now. I point up to the rafters at the plastic and Rico jumps for it, but can't quite reach it. He motions for me to come over. It's like we've agreed not to say anything. He lifts me up and I grab onto the rafter and pull myself up. The plastic is jammed under a piece of wood.

I'm shimmying over when I hear Rico say, "Shit," in a loud whisper.

A car. We hear a car door slam. I'm looking straight at Rico. He mouths the word, "Sorry," and takes off out of the garage.

I take a huge breath as light floods the garage. I

can see the lady walk back to the car and get inside. She drives in and turns off the motor. I can hear the radio. It's playing some country and western tune and the lady is singing the guitar part, going "darng nar nar nar da darng nar nar nar."

When the song finishes, the car turns off and the air around me goes all quiet. Too quiet. She gets out and shuts the door. Then she goes around to the back of the car and opens the hatch. She's been shopping. I can see right down her bags. She's got fruits and vegetables which are, like, only allowed in my house when Mom is on one of her healthy kicks. She's got a chicken and tomato sauce.

I'm drooling. I'm hiding like a fugitive up in the rafters and I've got to put my hand over my mouth to keep myself from dripping all over the lady.

She might see me when she closes the hatch. I close my eyes and wait for the sound of the car door shutting. After a while it does. She's gone. She forgot one bag of groceries on the floor.

I wait a couple of minutes for her to come back, but then I think I better make a run for it. I grab the plastic and lower myself down to the hood of the car. I slide down the back. I check out the grocery bag. It's got chips and ham in it. I have this huge urge to take it. She'll just think she forgot it at Loblaws. Elys did that once.

I grab it and go to the door. I pull on it and up it

comes. She forgot to lock it again.

"What the —" I look back and there she is. She didn't forget the groceries. I drop the grocery bag. She starts moving toward me.

"Sorry," I scream and take off like a bat out of hell. I run my legs off, with that plastic still stuffed under my arm. My lungs are burning and, as fast as I'm going, it doesn't feel like my feet are moving fast enough. I feel like I'm going to swallow my tongue, but I don't dare stop.

When I get to Bathurst Street, I close my eyes and run blind for a block. I hear my breath echoing through my whole body.

I run until I get a block away from my house. And then I look back.

There's nobody there.

I duck in between two stores to catch my breath. I have to go to the washroom. I still have the plastic. I can't believe I actually stole something. I shift the plastic from one sweaty armpit to the other. My whole side is wet with sweat. It feels cold with the wind blowing against it. I feel like I'm going to throw up. I feel like I'm going to faint. And, at the same time, I feel like I could run a hundred miles. It's like my feet want to keep going even though the rest of me wants to fall down.

My eyes are leaking. I wipe them with the back of my hand. How can I be such a suck? I could never be like Lucy. I could never be a thief. But I am one. In one day I've gone from being a decent kid to being a thief and a liar. I mean, I didn't exactly lie to Daphne, but I didn't tell her the whole truth.

I walk down behind the stores and puke by a tree in the parking lot.

I thought I was the good guy, the one who was owed, but I'm not. I'm a liar and a thief and I'm just like everyone else. Flat-face, ordinary, stupid-head, liar, thief, pervert, bat...

At least I'm still a bat.

14

I turn onto my street and see a police car outside my house. I'm crossing the road to go back up to the park when Mom comes out on the porch.

"Hey, where do you think you're going?"

I shrug.

"Get on in here. The police want to talk to you."

She doesn't look very happy. Who would when they just found out their only son was a thief? I put my head down and prepare to face the music.

I walk into the living room and there are two cops there, a man and a woman.

"You Terence?" the woman says. I nod.

"You know Lucille MacPhail?" the man says.

"Who?" That must be the lady I stole from.

"They mean your friend Lucy, Ter Bear." Oh. They aren't here about me. They're here about Lucy. Somehow I feel even more nervous than before.

I look at Mom and she has this curious look on her face. I look at the woman cop and nod.

"Her sister, Daphne MacPhail, says you saw her on the day she allegedly ran away."

"She said you guys couldn't do anything."

"Well, we'll see what we can do," the man says. I don't like the way he's talking. It's like he thinks he's

Columbo or something. I like the woman better. She's all business. "Maybe you can help us out?"

"Sure," I say. I'm talking to her, not to him. "I want you to find Lucy."

As I say it, I realize it's true. I don't want her to be in that cave, alone for another night. I didn't make that many sandwiches.

"Where was Lucy the last time you saw her?" the woman asks.

"Outside Loblaws two days ago."

"Is she your girlfriend?" the man asks. I knew I didn't like him.

"Please, he's a kid," my mom says.

"Just answer the question, Terence," the man cop says. I go and sit in the rocking chair.

"I don't know. I never kissed her, if that's what you mean."

"Don't get sarcastic with me, young man," the man says.

"We want to know whether Lucy told you anything about being upset. Are you good friends? Did she talk to you?"

I don't know what to say. Lucy did tell me why she ran away, but only after she left.

"She had lice," I say.

"What?" Mom says. "You never told me this, Terence." I shrug and rock in the chair.

"We know Lucille had lice. Is that why she ran

away? Or did you two, perhaps, get in a fight?" I now officially hate him.

"No. I helped Lucy. We're bats together." I shut up fast.

"Bats?" The woman cop catches it right away. I try to stop rocking, but I can't. "Do you belong to a street gang called the Bats?"

"What? Street gangs? Girlfriends? He's just a kid!" my mom screams.

"You'd be surprised, ma'am," the man cop says.

"Don't ma'am me, mister."

"Terence?" The woman squats down beside the rocking chair and puts her hand on the arm to steady it.

I wish I knew what to do. I don't think even Tom would know what to do in this situation.

"Lucy was upset about the lice and also because we cleaned her house the other day and nobody said anything."

"She ran away because no one thanked her for housekeeping? Sounds like my wife, heh, heh." The man cop is the only one who thinks his joke is funny. I feel sorry for his wife.

"Lucy ran away because nobody paid attention to anything she did. That house was a real mess and they didn't have anything to eat and nobody ever talked to her. It was like she didn't live there. The only person who knew she lived there was Daphne, and even she put a lock on her door to keep her out. How would you like to live in a place where it's like you're invisible? If she didn't leave the note, they probably wouldn't have known she'd run away."

My heart is pounding. I don't think I've ever talked like that to an adult before.

I hear a sound from Mom across the room. She looks real upset.

"What about these bats?" says the man cop. "How many of them are there?"

"Just me and Lucy." The guy thinks this is like television where every little thing is about some great big deal like gangs or drugs. It's like it can't be just about Lucy feeling bad.

"What do bats do?" says the police woman.

"Nothing," I say, slapping the arms of the chair. "We just are bats. That's all. We don't do anything. We be bats." They all look at me like I'm crazy. "You wouldn't understand. It's a kid thing." They all shift a bit and exhale, like they've been holding their breath waiting for me to say the right thing.

"What about this?" The man cop points to the plastic. He goes over and unfolds it. It makes a ton of noise. "What's this for?"

"Making a kite," I say, trying to keep my voice even. The police woman puts her hand on mine.

"Is that what bats do? Do they fly kites?" Instantly, I see my way out.

"I thought you used paper for kites," says the man cop.

"I wanted to make a big kite with a bat on it, because maybe Lucy would see it and come home. You know, like advertising for her to meet me." That's true, but I've already done that. The police woman looks me in the eye, pats my hand and stands up.

"That's a good idea, Terence. You do that." Both officers prepare to leave.

"And you let us know if your bat friend calls you or comes to your house," says the man cop.

"Her family really misses her and they want her home," says the police woman. I feel like telling her that they should have missed Lucy before she left. But then, you can't miss someone who is already there, can you? I look over at Mom. Maybe you can.

She leads the cops out and I hear the door close. She comes and sits on the sofa and looks at me. I rock.

"Where'd you get the plastic?" she asks. She's a way better cop than those two put together. There's no way I can lie to her.

"Rico's neighbor's garage," I say. I'm ready to tell her the whole thing. She looks at me for a long time like she wants to say something, but she doesn't.

*

I couldn't go out again last night because Mom wanted to watch television with me. I felt like she wanted to say something all night, but she wouldn't. I wished she would. I wanted to tell her all about Lucy, but my mouth wouldn't move. I kept opening it, but nothing came out.

Now she's gone to work and I'm rooting around the fridge to find something to take Lucy. We have one tomato and an onion. I make some Kraft Dinner and cut the onion and tomato into it. Lucy should get some vegetables.

When I get to the cave, there are sticks blocking up the entrance.

"Lucy?" I don't hear any movement in the cave. "Lucy?" I kick at the sticks. They come down easily enough. I crawl inside.

"Terence?" Lucy's voice is sleepy. A flashlight beams right in my face.

"The police were at my house last night. I brought you some Kraft Dinner."

Lucy props the flashlight in a corner. At the end of the cave I see a bunch of whittled branches. She has her kerchief off. I can see an orange sheen of stubble on her head. It looks like she dunked it in a vat of orange Kool-Aid.

"Your hair's growing back."

"Where were you? You said you were coming back. I waited and waited. A raccoon almost got me. I went out to go to the washroom and when I came back a bunch of raccoons were in here eating the

147

sandwiches. You said you were coming back. I waited all night, Terence." Her growly voice has been sawn in half. I feel like someone has sawn a hole in my stomach and stuffed it with straw.

"I brought you the plastic." She doesn't say anything. "I saw your sister in the park yesterday. She was crying. I don't think she's gone to work since you left. She was asking me about you."

"You didn't tell her anything?"

"Only that I saw you at Loblaws, but not about the spaghetti. I had to steal the plastic. I nearly got caught. Then I saw that police car at my house. They asked me why you ran away. I told them it was because no one paid attention to you. I didn't say anything about where you were."

Lucy seems to be listening, but she's looking at the sticks on the ground.

"I finished getting the branches ready for the kite frame. I had to go out and find some more pieces because a couple of them broke. We need something to write Save the Bats with. That's the right kind of plastic, though…I think. It's got paint splats on it. Oh, well."

Maybe she wasn't listening to me after all. Didn't she hear me say about the police?

"I had to put the sticks up to keep the raccoons out. It was so cold, I thought I was going to freeze to death. A bat's body temperature is supposed to lower inside the cave. There isn't enough room to hang upside-down here. That's probably why I was cold..."

"Maybe you should go home, Lucy. I'm bad at lying. If those cops come back, I don't know — "

"You can't tell them anything! Swear to me you won't. Swear, Terence. Swear on batdom!"

I don't think I can. Her eyes are so fierce. She looks so skinny and small. She should go home.

"How long will it take to make the kite?" Maybe if I help her get the kite done quickly, she'll go home after that.

Lucy sighs.

"That depends on when we get all the supplies." She unfolds the plastic. She looks a bit disappointed. Hell, I nearly got caught ripping that thing off. "Did you bring a measuring tape?" I pull the bag over and pull out the measuring tape and the string. "Good. Now all we need is some glue and paint."

I'm not stealing anything else. No way. Except... maybe Elys has some at the florist's. I could go there and come back, no problem. "If I bring them today, how long will it take?"

"I don't know, Terence. We'll just have to see." No. Once the kite is done she has to go home. That's the deal.

"You can't stay here forever." She opens the container of Kraft Dinner and grabs a fork.

"Why not?"

"Because you're not a bat, Lucy." I'm yelling. I think I have to yell so she'll hear me. "You're a girl. And your family's freaking, and the cops are looking for you, and I'll stop bringing food." She's gobbling the stuff up. How loud do I have to get? She holds a tomato up to the flashlight and then stuffs it in her mouth.

"So? There's always Loblaws. Bats find all their own food. Bats don't need anyone to take care of them."

I feel like throwing something. She makes me so angry. At the same time, watching her stuffing that Kraft Dinner in her face, with her bald head and knobby elbows sticking all out, I can't help feeling like I'd do anything for her.

"Are you my girlfriend?" The question pops out. Lucy stops eating and puts the container down.

"Are you doing all this stuff for me because you think I'm you're girlfriend?" I can't tell anything from her voice. I shake my head. "Good." She picks up the container and starts to eat again. She isn't looking at me anymore. It's like I'm invisible now. I guess she's not my girlfriend. I want to go home and stuff my head under a pillow.

"Do you like me?" I ask the floor because I can't look at her. I'm saying all the wrong things again. Stupid. I close my eyes.

I feel a hand on my head. I look up and Lucy is smiling at me. It's a smile like a new 18-speed mountain bike. It's a smile that goes all through me like a warm wind at the beach. She doesn't say anything. She just starts clicking.

Then I start clicking, too, only I'm no good at it. It's sort of a stuttering click. Then Lucy adds eeping to her clicking, like she's talking to me in bat. So I add some eeping.

"Eeep, eep, eep, click, click?"

"Click, click, eeep, eeeeeeeep."

Before long we're both jumping around in the cave, clicking, eeping and giggling. I'm not sure why, but acting this wild makes me feel like some part of Lucy is sane.

Only thing is, I think it's the bat part.

15

I go into the florist shop and the smell of flowers washes over me. It's like getting sprayed by one of those perfume ladies at the mall in how sudden the smell is. The door closes behind me and I hear a chime.

"Hey, there, sprout," Elys says, coming out of the back. She's got an apron on and everything. It's like she's been here forever and it's only her second day.

"Does that mean hello in florist?"

"Ha, ha. What can I do you for?"

"I'm making a kite and I was wondering if you maybe had some glue and tape and a marker or something that I could borrow." I say it fast just to get it out. Elys narrows her eyes at me.

"Another kite?" she says. I nod. "What happened to the one I gave you the other day? Why the sudden interest in kites? Aren't you supposed to be looking for your bat friend or something?"

She is too smart. I can tell by the look in her eye that she thinks she knows something.

"Your kite broke in the rain." That much is true. "I…I wanted to make a bat kite so that maybe I could fly it and Lucy would see it and come home." I'll stick with that story. It's almost true. Lucy will go home after we fly the Save the Bats kite. She has to.

"You think that she's somewhere where she could see a kite?" Elys says. I shrug. "Where are you going to fly this thing that you think she might see it?" I try shrugging again. "Well, this doesn't sound like a very well-thought-out plan, Ter. You know, I am new here. I could get into big trouble for giving away inventory."

"Yeah, like the guy's going to miss some tape."

"No. I just decided. I can't give you the stuff."

"You have to!" I blurt.

"No, Ter. I don't have to do anything. I know the police are on the case. They've been over to Russell's place several times already —"

"NO!" She stops for a second and eyes me. "He didn't. I mean, Russell's great. Lucy ran away. She left a note..."

"Well, you had to know that he's a suspect? A young girl is missing, Terence. It's an extremely serious situation, and your best idea is to fly a kite that she probably won't even see?" I'm still thinking about what she said about Russell. What has Rico been saying to the cops? Russell has nothing to do with anything.

"You have to give me the stuff. I don't have any money." Elys is shaking her head. "Come on. Please?"

"No." But she has to help me. I have to convince her.

"What else am I supposed to do? Sit around waiting for Lucy to show up? I think I know my friend, Elys. She might see the kite. You don't know. You aren't psychic."

"Where is she supposed to see it from?"

"The ravine."

She looks at me for a long minute. "Is Lucy in the ravine?"

She's trying to look in my eyes. I look down at my feet. My heart is pounding.

"Tell me where she is." I can feel my face getting red.

"You aren't going to give me the stuff?"

"No."

"Fine. I'll get it from Russell then. Thanks for nothing."

"Yeah, well, same to you."

I march out of the flower shop and look at Russell's building. He's on the ninth floor, I remember from riding the elevator with him.

There's only one R listed on the ninth floor. I push the button.

"Yes?" It's Russell's voice. Maybe he thinks I'm the police.

"It's Terence," I say.

"Who's that?"

"Lucy's friend," I say. He buzzes me in.

When I get off the elevator, I see his head poking

into the hall. I wave and he puts his head back in. I get to the door and can see behind him into the living room.

His place is painted all different colors. Like the living room is orange and the kitchen is blue. I don't know what I was expecting, but this... it's like something out of a magazine. It's the opposite of Lucy's place in how clean it is. There's music going, too. Old cowboy songs, not country music like the kind Elys hates, but something about sleeping under the stars and a cold wind. And there are bookshelves everywhere. And something else...

"You don't have a television?"

"What? Oh, no," he says. Out the window you can see across to the ravine. "Can I help you with something, Terence?"

Now I don't really know what I'm here for. If I ask for the kite stuff he'll be on to me in a flash. Anyone who can think three moves ahead is going to be able to figure this thing out...

I sit down and Russell stands up. He looks at me and then out the window. He must be really worried about Lucy.

Look at what Lucy's made me do now. All these people worried about her and getting in trouble because of her. Why didn't she ask Russell for help? Why didn't she come to my house? Why wouldn't she let Elys buy her some spaghetti?

Russell's looking out the window and so am I.

"I looked for you in the park the other day but you weren't there," I say. He looks out the window and then sits on the couch.

"I haven't been feeling well. I've been busy." I can see where the police might be suspicious of him. Shy guys always get a bad rap. It's not that we don't want to talk to people. It's just everything that comes out of our mouths sounds stupid. But I know Russell isn't stupid. He just looks so guilty. I even think he looks guilty and I *know* he isn't. How must it feel to have a whole neighborhood thinking you're a pervert? Russell keeps blinking.

I have to stop this. It is up to me to stop this.

How am I going to get Lucy home? Even if we finish the kite today, it's no guarantee she'll come back. I wonder what Tom would do? Nothing. Tom would pretend it wasn't his problem. Tom would ask *me* what to do. That's right. I never thought of that before.

What would I do then? Who would I ask what to do?

"If you had a friend..." I start. Russell looks up at me. I'm tempted to stop, but I've started already. "If you had a friend who was in trouble and said she didn't want help, but you knew she needed it, but she asked you not to tell anybody, what would you do?"

He's got this huge smile on his face. It's like I just told him about buried treasure.

"You know where Lucy is, don't you?" he says. He's looking at me straight over those humongous glasses of his.

I wait a few seconds and then shake my head. I feel suddenly heavier, like someone just loaded ten bowling balls on my shoulders. Russell's face falls.

I feel the water rising in my eyes. I open my mouth to tell him. I want to say something, but I can't. It's like sitting with Mom watching television the other night, only it's a thousand times worse, like, if I speak, bugs will come out. I sit there trying not to cry and thinking about how I'm all full of bugs, like a bat, only I can't be a bat. Bats don't lie.

Finally, Russell stands up. He walks over to the window and looks out.

"Thanks for coming by, Terence."

I stand up. He wants me to go.

He knows I'm a liar and he's not going to help me.

My promise to Lucy has made me a liar. The only way to make up for it is to bring her home. She's coming if I have to drag her by her feet. It's all up to me now. I want to come clean. I want to be bug free.

I pass through Wells Hill Park. Rico and Daphne are on the bench under the picnic table. I have to try to look fine now. I can't help thinking how everything gets messed up by people pretending to feel one way when they feel another. That's how gaps are born. Never mind. I can do it this one last time.

"Hi," I say. They both barely look up. Rico takes a slug off his Big Gulp and offers it to Daphne. She shakes her head. I wait for him to offer it to me, but I guess I don't count because I'm a guy. "Any news yet?"

Daphne sighs and shakes her head. She's got huge circles under her eyes. I should tell her now. I could just say something and it would be all over. I'm dying to say something.

"The news is there is no news," says Rico, like he's in charge of the whole investigation. Man, he burns me up.

"Oh, shut up, Rico," Daphne says. She must be tired of him, too. She smiles. "We'll let you know if we hear anything, Terence." I start walking away. Every step I take away from Daphne makes the gap in my stomach grow ten times larger. I didn't know it was possible to feel this bad. I start running. I feel too heavy for my feet, but they carry me anyway. Away, away, away.

16

"Lucy!" I burst into the cave.

"Careful, careful, careful," she screams. I back up against the side.

She's got the kite all laid out. The sticks are all strung together and the plastic's over top of the whole works. She has the kite book open by her feet. She's copied the design from a picture. It shows a guy with water skis hanging from a kite, sort of like a hang-glider. Underneath, the words say Alphonso Woodall of Cleveland tried to be flown from a kite in 1959 for the television show "You Asked For It" — only the kite got caught in a cross draft and he plummeted fifty feet. Alphonso ended up with a broken leg and two broken heels.

I'm scared for Lucy.

The wings of the bat kite fill the whole cave. The branches for Lucy to hang from run along the bottom. I'm not sure they will hold her weight. The picture of Alphonso Woodall, kite-rider, shows him wearing a helmet and a special flight suit.

I have to admit that she's done a really good job, though. The thing looks like it just might work. Wouldn't it be something to watch her soar onto Russell's balcony?

Lucy's smiling and has this glow of pride all over her. I wish I could be happy for her.

One thing's for sure. The kite's almost done. There's no talking her out of it now.

"Click, click, eep, eep. She sure is some beauty," I say.

"Did you bring the stuff?"

"I…no."

She looks up at me and shakes her head in disappointment. Then she walks over to her knapsack, picks it up and chucks it at me. Spray paint, tape, glue — all the stuff she asked me for.

"Where'd you get all this?" She doesn't answer. "You stole it, didn't you?"

"I couldn't wait on you all day, Terence. And, as it turns out, it's a good thing I didn't. It wasn't easy, either. I had to get all that stuff in the bag without the hardware guy seeing. I couldn't get the spray paint until some lady came in to yell at him about her new keys not fitting her lock. But, a bat's gotta do what a bat's gotta do. And you don't always come when you say you're going to."

My hands go into fists at my sides. I'm so angry, I can't even talk. She has no idea what I've gone through for her, what everyone is going through for her.

I turn to leave. Let her crash that thing into the side of the hill. At least they'll find her then. All busted up…I swallow my pride and pick up the glue.

"So looks like all we have to do is glue the edges over and reinforce the sticks with tape, right?" I clap my hands and get busy.

Lucy grabs the glue bottle from me.

"This is a very delicate operation. You'd better let me handle it." She's growling at me. It's like I've done something wrong. Fine, I'm mad at her, too. I watch her put a stick in the glue bottle and smear it along the flap of plastic. She folds it over, presses it down and smooths it out.

"Put some tape here," she says. I lean down and put the masking tape along the glued fold to make it extra secure. Maybe if I just shut up we'll be done real fast and out of here.

Lucy puts some glue over the spots where the sticks cross.

"There. Now we just have to wait for it to dry," she says.

"Then we spray paint it. Then you fly it. Then you go home." I wait for her to say something, but she's busy playing with the glue around the sticks. Her head looks like a peach. Half of me wants to kiss it and the other half wants to put it in a headlock and drag it home. I don't want a girlfriend if she's going to be as stubborn as this.

"After we fly the kite, we go home. Right, Lucy? Eep, eep?"

"We'll see." She doesn't even look at me when she says it. I can feel her not caring about anything I say. I can feel her not-caring attitude bouncing off her like a high-frequency bat echo.

My palms begin to sweat. What if I can't get her out of here? I don't want to tell the police, but I'll have to. She's made me lie long enough.

"What do you mean? You said! You said you'd go home once the kite is done. I shouldn't even let you do it. You don't have a helmet or anything. What if you crash?"

"You aren't the boss of me." Lucy turns on me with that voice and those eyes. She sounds like shoveled gravel. "Why don't you just leave me alone? Why don't you go home? It's none of your business what I do. I don't need you." I can see tears coming up in her eyes but they won't fall. She is so stubborn.

"Why are you so mad at me?" I can hear a crack in my voice. "I thought I was a bat, too. You said —"

"People say things all the time. It doesn't mean anything. People are liars. They say they're doing something for you, or they're your friend, but it's just to make themselves feel better." She goes and sits in the corner, in the dark where I can hardly see her.

My whole body feels weak with sadness.

"Everyone lies," she says. "Only dead people don't lie." This must be what it feels like when your heart is breaking. I want to leave the cave and run to

Elys. But instead, I find myself crawling to sit beside Lucy.

"Do you mean Timber doesn't lie?"

At the sound of Timber's name, Lucy starts wailing. I have never heard such a sound in all my life. I put my arm around her and she cries into my baggy T-shirt. I can feel her getting snot on it, too, but I don't care. It is like a whole bunch of sadness is flying out of her and out of the cave on the backs of angel bats.

I hold her bald head and feel the bristles of her growing-back hair scratch the palm of my hand. If hair can grow back, maybe hearts can, too.

It's a good ten minutes before Lucy stops crying enough to catch her breath. I can feel things changing already.

"Timber was a good friend of yours," I say. "Daphne told me." Lucy nods but doesn't open her eyes. She's still breathing funny.

"She was my best friend. The best ever. So I don't know why…"

Lucy kicks the kite. The branches crack loudly as she stomps on them. I cover my ears. Now she'll never finish it! She jumps up and down on it. I want to yell stop but it's too late. The kite's already ruined. Lucy's tearing at the plastic with her hands. I'm scared. I think Lucy's going crazy. I should go get someone but I can't leave her alone.

Lucy is stuffing the dead kite into the entrance to the cave. She's lying on the floor of the cave and pounding it out the opening with her feet. I watch her do it. It sure is a small opening. Even broken, the kite takes a lot of effort to get out.

Something clicks inside my head and I can't help giggling. Maybe it's because I'm nervous. Lucy stops stomping and looks at me. I didn't even think she knew I was still here. I'm terrified of what she's going to do to me, but I can't help it anymore. I'm laughing. I'm hysterical.

"What?" she says. Her voice is calmer now. She looks angry at me. "What is it?"

I'm trying not to laugh. I swear. But I look at her being angry at me and I can't help breaking up. She bangs her hand against the top of the cave and some dust comes down. I fall down on my back laughing.

"Terence! What are you laughing at?" I point at the door.

"I don't know how we thought we were going to get that kite out the door in one piece." I manage to get the words out between laughs.

Lucy gives one more stiff kick to the plastic jammed in the mouth of the cave. She pounds it with her feet a few more times.

Then she starts laughing, too. She laughs and kicks at the plastic. I go over and help her. We kick at it and kick at it, like we're trying to kill it, like you can kill plastic by stomping on its head. Our feet are going so fast, it's like those cartoon feet on that Tasmanian Devil guy, where you can't even see his feet, that's how fast they're going.

Then the plastic is all the way out the door and we just keep on kicking because it's fun.

I look over at Lucy and she looks at me and we both stop and just look at each other for a while.

And I get this strange feeling.

It's like when I used to have these nightmares about a crocodile in my bed, and I'd go to Mom's room and crawl under the covers and go to sleep feeling safe. It's just that exact feeling, of knowing that even though there's a crocodile in *your* bed, it doesn't meant there's crocodiles everywhere you go.

It's like somehow me and Lucy just closed a big gap full of nightmares.

17

I turn around and look out the cave. It's a beautiful sunny day. That didn't matter to me five minutes ago, and now it's like…it's like the whole world. Lucy turns around and pokes her head out, too. We both have to squint a bit. I push the plastic out of the way so we can see farther.

"Here!" someone shouts.

I want to hide, but then — it's over. I know it's over. Lucy starts to crawl back into the cave but I hold her by the arm.

"Lucy," I say. "I think the kite's done now." She nods, peels my hand off her arm and crawls out of the cave.

"Is that where you've been hiding out?"

It's Russell. I should have known. I crawl out of the cave and brush off my knees. Russell is hugging Lucy.

"Come on, now. It's time to go home."

"How did you know where I was?" she asks. I grit my teeth.

"Well, I'm afraid Terence isn't as good at hiding as you are."

"Lucy! Hey, she's over here." Daphne and Rico appear at the edge of the hill and Daphne starts running down sideways. She can't go too fast or she'll fall. That's one killer hill.

I look down at the broken plastic kite and think how close I came to letting Lucy try to fly.

Russell must have followed me. He must have collected Daphne and Rico on his way through the park. If I hadn't run all the way from Wells Hill to the ravine, they probably would have found us right away.

Now Lucy is in her sister's arms.

"Thank God. Thank God," Daphne keeps saying. "I am so sorry, Lucy." And then, "Don't you ever run away again. We thought..."

I go back into the cave because I can't stand all that corny crud. It's just like television, only worse, because it's three-dimensional.

I start gathering up Lucy's stuff and Elys sticks her head in the cave.

"Gotcha!" she says and pokes me in the arm. "I *knew* you were coming here, and when Russell called...wow. Is this where she was?"

I should have known it was too easy getting out of the florist shop.

"And you knew all this time?" she says. I keep still. "Why didn't you tell anyone, Terence?"

"I promised Lucy. If she didn't come with me today, I was going to tell."

"Do you realize what could have happened? She was out here alone for three nights. You can't leave a friend in a dangerous position, even if she asks you to. You have to take care of your friends when they're in trouble like this. You have to say something."

"How do you know how to help someone?" I spit out. "No one was taking care of Lucy at home. No one cared about her until she ran away. Maybe I was helping her. Seems like everyone cares now."

Elys grabs my wrist. I try not to look at her. Adults think they know everything. Just because she's got a job, now she thinks she's Queen of the World Smartypants.

"You don't know what it's like to think that maybe your kid is dead, Ter. She didn't even tell her parents she had lice. Don't you think she could have given them the chance to make good?"

"But why should she have to? They should have known. They should have been paying attention."

Elys looks in my eyes and then folds me into a hug. She softens right up.

"That's right. They should have been paying attention."

I don't know why, but I start crying. Elys hugs me tighter. "Maybe people don't pay enough attention to the important things. We get preoccupied. It's bad and wrong — and it happens all the time. It shouldn't, but it does. That's why you need to learn how to YELL."

She actually yells when she says that. It echoes all over the cave.

Elys is cool, like a bat.

Her hollering makes me realize where I am. Even though it's better that everyone knows where Lucy is, I'm going to miss our secret hideout. I wonder how a bat like Lucy will survive outside her cave.

I wipe my eyes and start packing stuff up in the knapsack. Elys is looking at the kite book.

"You really were making a kite, weren't you?"

"Lucy was. She was going to ride it all over town. She had it all built. It looked like it was going to work, too. See?" I point to the mess in the mouth of the cave. Elys picks up one of the branches. You can tell from the size of the branch how sturdy the thing would have been.

"She would've killed herself."

"I wasn't going to let her do it, Elys."

"How did you stop her?"

"It's a long story. She kind of stopped herself."

"Tell me."

I shake my head.

"Nope. Bats don't rat on bats."

We crawl outside and everyone is standing around talking. It's like a wedding reception or something.

Rico rubs Lucy on the head and says, "What happened to your hair, Loser?"

"Get your hands off me, Moran."

At least Lucy's sane enough to still hate Rico.

Those two cops come down the path and Russell goes out to meet them. He points up to the cave, then over at Lucy and next, at me. I feel myself blush hard. The police woman comes over to us.

"You all right?" she asks Lucy.

"Yeah, I guess," says Lucy. Daphne puts her arms around her again.

"You stayed in there?" the cop motions toward the cave. Lucy nods. "Nobody put you there? Nobody forced you to do anything?"

"No. I put me there."

The police woman goes and pulls the man cop aside. Then he wanders over.

"You know this man?" He motions at Russell.

"Yeah. That's Russell," says Lucy. You can tell from her eyes that she's just cluing in to what's been going on while she's been holed up in the cave.

"Is he in trouble because I ran away?" Lucy looks at me. "Did I get Russell in trouble?"

The cop looks over at Rico. Lucy's looking at everyone looking at Rico.

"Not exactly, Lucy," I say. "I think Rico got Russell in trouble. You shouldn't have run away, but Rico was the one who told them he thought Russell was a..." I can't say it with Russell standing here.

"A what? What did you tell them, Moran?" she yells at Rico.

Rico looks like he wants to take off, but the

police man has him by the arm.

"I think you'd better tell them, Rico," says the cop. "And then you'd best apologize to the man."

Rico's big face is all tight, and I can tell he's blinking back tears. But he won't open his mouth.

"'fess up, Rico," I say. He looks at me.

"I called him a pervert, okay? Satisfied?"

"I'm not satisfied," says the police man. I'm beginning to like him a little. "Are you satisfied?" he asks Russell.

Russell has his hand on his chin. He looks like he could throw boulders with his eyes, he's so angry.

"No," he almost whispers. His being so quiet makes him sound even angrier.

"Apologize," the cop says to Rico. Rico looks up at the cop.

"I'm sorry," he says.

"Not to me," says the cop. "To him." He points at Russell. Rico looks up at Russell and bursts into tears.

"I'm so sorry, mister." He wipes his nose with the back of his arm. He's still looking Russell straight in the eye. "I didn't think, mister. I'm sorry."

Russell softens up, slowly, while Rico bawls. Finally, the cop lets go of his arm.

"I think it's time we all went home," says Russell.

We all start heading out of the ravine. All except for Rico. I wouldn't mind leaving him there, but

Russell calls back for him. "Come along, Rico."

Rico catches up, but not all the way. He tags behind us a bit as we make our way up to the street.

"By the way," Elys whispers in my ear, "I phoned your mom. She should be home by now." I look up at her and she gives me this huge, evil, no-teeth smile.

We all walk together toward Wells Hill Park. I feel like it's been a million years since I was here.

Tom will be home in a couple of weeks. It doesn't seem like a lot of time anymore. I mean, I want to spend more time with Lucy before he gets back. I want to play her at chess.

How am I going to explain to Tom how a bald girl could be so beautiful? He'll never believe all this stuff. Even if he does, he'll pretend like it's no big deal. I don't think he could stand to know that life goes on without him.

When we get to where it's time to split ways, Lucy breaks away from Daphne and the cops and comes over to me. She seems like another person already. I feel kind of embarrassed.

"Well, anyway, thanks," she says. She puts out her hand for me to shake. I take it. I have the strangest urge to kiss her, like I could just do it and get away with it and not have it be any big deal.

I give her a huge smile instead. I'll kiss her later. I'll kiss her next week. I'll kiss her sometime when it's just her and me.

"You're welcome," I say.

"I still want to make the Save the Bat kite. We'll do it properly this time. We'll, like, read books and stuff. You'll help, right?"

I nod. She leans forward toward my ear. I feel a chill run down my back. Then she whispers, "Eep, eep, eep." She turns and runs back to Daphne and the cops.

You can't take the bat out of Lucy.

I wonder if there's enough of Lucy that's human to keep her from flying off again. She's getting a police escort home to her parents, but what happens then?

I watch Daphne put her arm around her sister and make for home. Russell and Rico are going that way, too. They're walking beside each other, but neither of them is talking. The cops pull up the rear.

Elys and I watch them all go until there's nothing more to watch. Then we start walking home.

"Don't worry," Elys says. "Lucy will be all right."

"How do you know?"

"She's got you, doesn't she? Friends take care of friends. And you're a good friend, Terence."

The sun sifts through the branches that hang over the street. I watch my shadow move slowly down the road. I feel like I'm chained to my shadow, like there is a dark part of me — a bat part of me — that will follow me from now on, no matter where I go.

Elys sighs and throws her arm over my shoulders. It should weigh me down even more, but it doesn't. It makes me feel so light, like if I opened my arms, I could fly.